CHILLS

ALEX POOLE

First published in Great Britain as a softback original in 2022

Copyright © Alex Poole

The moral right of this author has been asserted.

Typeset in Dante MT Std

Editing, design, typesetting and publishing by UK Book Publishing

www.ukbookpublishing.com

ISBN: 978-1-915338-17-4

CHILLS

CHAPTER ONE

Crack...
Crack, crunch...

Along trail of polar ice broke apart under its hull as the HMS *Platinum* smashed through the polar north's frigid landscape. Bone-chilling winds lashed at the exterior of the icebreaker and howled in protest of its advancement, failing to deter the massive ship from pressing forward in pursuit of its objective. At the helm, surrounded by the noise and general busyness of sailors and navigators at work, a thin plume of steam rose from the gently shaking tea flask of a young blond-haired researcher. On his way to survey a rare and unusual specimen, which had been contained and was awaiting his arrival.

'We will be arriving within sledding distance of Base Neptune shortly, and might I add, it has been a pleasure to be of service in the interest of making history today, Mr Voe, sir,' came the familiar voice of the ship's captain from behind its wheel. The researcher looked up at the captain from over the rim of his flask and smiled. 'You have my thanks for taking me and the rest of the team all this way to meet with our associates at Neptune. This has been a long time coming, I have a strong feeling that everything is going to pay off marvelously; we will indeed be making history.'

1

Approaching its destination, the hulking icebreaker began to slow down, gradually coming to a rest. It remained stationary, in the freezing water, for a couple of hours before movement could be seen on the starboard side and a ramp began to descend onto the flat, solid ice below. When it was fully deployed five men began their descent, all were clad in thermal jackets and face protection to keep them safe in the freezing weather. They were followed by a small escort of sled handlers with their dogs. The accompanying sound of grinding winches and mechanisms, lowering the first of the research team's sleds down onto the ice spooked the already excited canines, making them even harder to handle. When each of the three sleds were finally on the ground, stocked up and hooked onto the harnesses of the animals, the trio pushed off, travelling north through the harsh wind towards the distant research base which peeked out on the horizon, currently only a mere grey speck in an ocean of cold white snow.

For the entire duration of the journey, the dogs pulled and veered off course, and the constant wrangling was starting to become a serious pain for the entire team. At a point midway along their journey, Andrew Voe, the lead researcher of his group, eager to see his life's work realised, briefly pulled down the lenses of his snow goggles to get a better look at the shapes surrounding the exterior of the metal walls of Base Neptune; they eventually formed into the recognisable appearances of trucks, diggers and drilling equipment, as well as the dishes of communication arrays and antennae as they approached. Andrew almost didn't take notice at first, but after a few taps on his shoulder he recognised that his colleague, an esteemed geneticist sitting to the right of him, wanted to say something, and so he leaned in and pulled back the earflap on his hat to the side facing him.

'I was trying to say, are you positively sure about this... investor? I know we're making a breakthrough that could well net us some serious awards in our field but I haven't heard anything good about him. I'm saying that I don't think he's trustworthy.'

Andrew withdrew slightly at the query, contemplating his answer, and then leaned back in again.

'If it wasn't for him, none of us would be here and I know that it's a hard pill to swallow but if we didn't have somebody with the resources to secure this finding first then I don't want to think about what could happen if this discovery fell into the hands of somebody less... how should I put it... morally just?'

'I'm pointing out that I don't completely trust him, the whole private military firm, the shady background. I agree that we need to have this place protected and his involvement is helping substantially in that regard but I can't help but feel like this is going to cost us. I can feel it in my gut.'

'Well Harvey, he has a reputation to keep too. If he was the morally unjust sort he would have just taken all of the findings there and left already, sold them off to the highest bidder, but as you can see by the activity up there, he has chosen to stick around. Anyway, we'll be at the research base soon, we'll meet up with the investor and you can get a nice mug of coffee for your gut while I handle him until we're done. After that, we can see what we came here for and lastly, pack up and go home so that we can spend the rest of our lives taking autographs and having students write essays about us. Does that sound good?'

With a muffled grunt, Andrew's colleague returned to his sitting position and the pair travelled the rest of the way in silence until they had reached the foot of a large metal dome which made up the main complex of the Research Base and its surrounding cabins where they were greeted by a number of personnel from the base. Some had handheld radios, binoculars or equipment for dealing with the arctic conditions but the one thing they all shared, was that they were all armed. When the sleds were finished being unloaded and the research team was given a security check by the guards, the doors to the metal dome opened up and the team was escorted inside.

Harvey turned to him with a worried look as they both travelled with the rest of the group down a corridor within the first inner layer of the building which was lined with numerous pipes and doors to various parts of the facility.

'I mean, are the guns really necessary? I can understand that there are a lot of people who would want to get their hands on what you have found but how many do you think are willing, and have the resources, to come out all this way to get it?'

Andrew returned the look with a tired expression.

'Russia, China, the States. Look, they're on our side, they won't be pointing anything at us so if anything, I'd say that I feel doubly safe here.'

Despite Andrew's attempt to relieve the situation, his partner remained hesitant.

'And this sample that they say they have found... You haven't told me much about it, only that it came from something which was living... And something about "compatibility"?'

'Ah-ha, yes, I gave them the go-ahead to begin testing on it to figure out what we can learn from it and right away we got some rather intriguing results.'

'Which are?'

'Which are: its DNA, cell structure, everything about the composition of the tissue was unique. Cross-referencing found no similar matches anywhere else in the world. And then there's "compatibility".'

As Andrew's explanation went on, his body language was becoming increasingly pronounced, as if he was working up to something big. This only seemed to exacerbate the distrust that his colleague was clearly feeling.

'It's compatible with anything... Or at least it should be. We were never able to find a whole specimen of the creature that it came from, but in theory, owing to the flexibility of its genetic structure, there is the great possibility that we could restore it to what it originally looked like. Just like those pipe dreams of restoring the dinosaurs from amber, but this time it could be realistically feasible. I am well aware that this is something that needs to be seen to be believed, which is precisely why I have chosen to take you with me to see it for yourself.'

Harvey's worry was now only weighed down with a growing doubt as to his associate's credibility.

'Mr Voe, what you're saying right now is impossible. I'm sorry to say this to you because I know full well how hard you strived to get to this point, but what you're talking about... it just doesn't happen in reality. If its biology is different to anything else on the planet then it can't possibly be compatible with anything else, it's completely contradictory... I just can't help but keep feeling like this specimen that's been found is going to turn out to be just a load of nothing; a big red herring, and when the investor and his gunmen find that out for themselves then we're going to be in very deep water. I'm sorry, but if this is anything like fossils and amber, then a bunch of bloodthirsty mercenaries are not going to treat us with the slightest bit of gratitude.'

'Okay, okay, I may be getting way ahead of myself just a little bit but, I mean, it's a whole new creature. The test results that came back to me showed things that I didn't even think were possible and the more reports that came through about it, the more I wanted to come out here to see it for myself. I trust you and think that you would know how to handle this kind of data. Your support could take all of us on the team a big step towards, perhaps, achieving something that the greatest of the great would be proud of had they discovered it themselves. Just one more room ahead and we'll be in the sample chamber and you can see it for yourself. I know that it can live up to the expectations that I've set out for you...'

And there it was.

Suspended in a large and complicated-looking pod on the far side of a room lined with desks holding lab equipment of all shapes and sizes. Harvey's eyes widened upon seeing the specimen. Andrew simply grinned smugly. The sample was surrounded by a scene like something out of an alien autopsy. A large chunk of what could be assumed to be part of a torso with a large, bear-like arm attached to one side, displayed within the pod's glass window, submerged in a preservative liquid and held in place by five delicate metal arms. The specimen appeared to have small, fish-like scales which were bone-white in colour. Currently there were a pair of researchers in pristine white lab coats looking in through the glass, one of them noticeably larger-built than the other, who was keying notes into a tablet.

'So... First impressions?'

Andrew's research partner turned to him, completely dumbfounded.

'That can't be real. I'm absolutely sure you're having me on now.'

'Oh, I can assure you that what you're seeing is no illusion. "This" is what we found under the ice. Shall we take a closer look?'

Harvey shrugged.

'Well alright, I'll humor you and go in with the assumption that this could be real, but when I get that thing under a microscope and all I see is plastic, I'll be the one who's laughing.'

Andrew stepped back slightly and folded his arms. 'I'm game if you're willing to bet on that.'

Harvey glanced over to the pod and then back to Andrew, a smirk gradually surfacing from his ocean of worry and distrust.

'Oh, I would bet my career on it.'

When the two scientists split off from their group and approached the pod, the larger of the two men who were currently studying it, turned to them and waved off the other, who nodded politely and scurried off to a table further away from them. Andrew looked up at him with a warm expression and extended a hand.

'Maxwell my friend, apologies that I didn't recognise you out of uniform. It's a pleasure to meet the man who made this all happen.'

'No, no, the pleasure it all mine. This has been like a lovely holiday, coming out here and getting to spend quality time with the lab folk and this...'

Maxwell tapped the pod's window a few times.

'Marvelous specimen you've got here.'

7

'We don't really have a set-in-stone name for it yet but, from what I've seen, we should be able to reverse-engineer it to see what the whole thing looked like, then we will probably have a better idea on what to name it. When we do though you can bet that it's going to be damn impressive.'

The man in the lab coat then turned his attention towards Andrew's partner and the two exchanged a handshake.

'And you must be Doctor Harvey Lilac. Mr Andrew here tells me that with you on the job, putting the pieces together on this mystery meat we've got here should be a piece of cake.'

Harvey let go of Maxwell's hand and stuttered slightly.

'Oh, um… Yes, with the right tools for the job I should be able to get a very accurate analysis of our specimen and… Might I ask, you're the investor for the project?'

'That's right, Maxwell Adams - chief investor and CEO of Black Mamba Excursions, I'm sure you've heard all about me.'

'Erm, yes… the excursions in Afghanistan and… the…'

Maxwell raised his eyebrow slightly at the mention of the subject but turned it into a chuckle. Harvey tried hard not to cringe, having foolishly chosen to test the investor's amiability with the mention of a topic that had muddied his hands in controversy.

'Ah, that's all water under the bridge now. Coming here in person proves that I have much better things to be doing with my time and money, don't I?'

Something about the way that Maxwell was grinning at the both of them was hard not to perceive as unnerving.

'In any case, I've been getting involved with a good deal of the management and directing here, and would like for you to follow me for a moment. I'll take you to see where we found it, and then we can head over to B Lab where they're doing all the fun stuff.'

As Andrew and his associate started to follow the investor out towards a nearby exit, Harvey took one last look into the pod which held the mysterious body. The skin of the subject was more than just a stunning ivory hue, it was somewhat translucent; veins and bone structure could be vaguely made out beneath its surface, and around the area where the flesh was sheared off there were signs of large bite marks, uncharacteristic of any animal that Harvey had studied, where the skin had been torn as if by many sharp hooks. It would have been impossible to tell exactly what had killed it; Harvey's best guess was that it must have been a bear of some sort. The last thing that he noticed briefly was that the end of the specimen's arm was oddly shaped. Was one of its fingers more shaped like a thumb? Like what humans have? It jutted out at an angle that suggested it could be... Still, each of its fingers was tipped with the kind of wickedly sharp claws that could only belong to an animal. Harvey was left to ponder what he had seen as Andrew noticed him lagging behind and signaled him to hurry up.

Maxwell Adams directed the two researchers through another short corridor and into a room with a large pressure-sealed door, and a small number of vehicles for transporting equipment and samples to and from the area beyond. After passing through this room, they came to an office-like space with a large, glass observation screen which showed what lay beyond the bulkhead in the previous room.

The room which the observatory looked out on was taken up almost entirely by an enormous crater in the ice, drilled out and tunneled into, with rows of lights and cables going deep into it until they disappeared from view.

Maxwell pulled up a seat and instructed the other two to do the same.

'So, a little backstory on this place. In 1991, Mr Daniel Voe, God rest his soul, goes out into the arctic to conduct a little survey of, what was then believed to be, a nigh-impenetrable sheet of solid rock under the ice, so thick that they said back then, that there was next to no hope of any tunneling equipment getting through safely. Any plans to find out what was under it since then had been met with complete failure. That is until two years ago when you, Mr Voe's dear son, found a weak point in the ice; drills arrive with the first and second batch of tunneling teams and get to work... And what do they find after drilling for three days straight, but a bunch of mystery tunnels. Nobody knows what made them and the pictures show that they're not naturally formed. So, how did they get here?'

Maxwell passed a picture to the other two showing a crew of tunnellers cramped into one of the glacial caves with walls and floor carved from solid ice, gathered around the specimen which was now inside the pod. It was lying on the ground along with a lot of blood still leaking from it, staining the ice around it a deep red and seeming to create odd shapes, almost like bubbles in the frozen tunnel floor.

'Since then, we took over the operation here and brought it back, then we did a bunch of tests with some... really, very interesting outcomes.'

Harvey scratched his head as he studied the picture and then passed it over to Andrew before speaking.

'How far down did you say the tunneling team went before they found these structures? From this picture it almost looks as if the specimen had died not long before it was taken.'

'Just less than 400 metres, and it does, doesn't it? We still don't know what caused that but it's not really much of our concern anymore. Now what the subject has been providing for us in B Lab is really something quite special. Let's continue on.'

There was a longer journey this time between the observatory and the next destination within Base Neptune that the investor was taking them to, and some way along the journey Harvey once again pulled on Andrew's sleeve.

'Look Andrew, he said that whatever did that isn't really their concern, but how could it not be? I saw the marks on that thing and I would not like to meet whatever caused it.'

Andrew sighed and gave an expression that said "oh really?"

'Dear me... Not ten minutes ago you were telling me that you didn't even think that it was real. Are you starting to have doubts Doctor Lilac?'

'No, damnit, no... I bet on this, I'm not going to back down now. I'm just worried that there would be a security concern in case there is something down there, is all.'

'Monsters under the ice?' Andrew suggested slyly.

'Please, that's childish. It could be bears, or something else we already know of, more likely.'

'Well, I'm sure that whatever it is, if it comes back, the security here is more than prepared to deal with it. Wild animals don't tend to fare very well when it comes to automatic rifles after all.'

'I would rather it didn't come to that.'

Andrew turned his attention back to Maxwell as they passed another set of rooms filled with lab staff and tables.

'So, I take it that B Lab is where the samples are being processed for the trial reports I've been reading about over e-mail?' Andrew asked the investor, hovering just behind him.

'That and a whole lot more. In fact, we have some results which we'd decided to keep under wraps until you both arrived in person. It's a bit of a shame that we couldn't give you the whole picture right away but we had to take precautions in case of any unfortunate data breaches. Still, there's nothing better than the surprise of finding out that progress is going even better than what you heard back in jolly old Blighty. Am I right?'

'Well, if things are going even better, then I'm very excited to find out just how much better they can get.'

'Good, and you'll be pleased to know then, that B wing labs is just around the corner, so the long wait is over, I'm sure you will be suitably impressed.'

After heading in through a set of double-doors, the trio entered into a room which was clustered with many different kinds of testing equipment, large and intricate machines, microscopes, beakers, and, along one side of the room behind a plastic screen, was what looked like an MRI machine, along with a board which held a number of x-ray prints pinned to it. Maxwell led them over to a table where a lab technician was slotting in a sample plate under one of the microscopes fitted with a number of different lenses.

'Excuse us please but could we take a look at your work for a moment?'

'Oh, of course Mr Adams, sir, everything is set up.'

With that, the technician moved away quietly and joined with another on a separate table. Maxwell gently put his hands around the microscope and lifted it off of the table.

'Are you sure we should be moving it? I mean, this is surely an expensive piece of equipment?'

Maxwell laughed at the question from Andrew.

'I'm sure they won't mind, I'm very careful with this kind of stuff. I'm the one who paid for most of this junk anyway, we're just moving our example piece to somewhere a bit quieter... Hey, you there! Could you hold open that door, please!?'

The lab staff who Maxwell had shouted at stopped dead in the middle of what he was doing and rushed over to open the door to a smaller room, holding it open while Maxwell walked in, cradling the heavy microscope in his arms. Andrew and Harvey followed suit and shut the door behind them as Maxwell placed it on the table.

He turned to Dr Lilac and offered him a chair, which he took and looked to Andrew expectantly. In this time, Maxwell left the table momentarily and headed off towards another one further down, where a coffee machine was stationed along with a tube filled with paper cups.

'So Doctor, here's the moment of truth, what we have here is a sample taken from the specimen in A wing and there should be nobody to interrupt us in here. The stage is yours, so to speak.'

'Alright, let me just get this adjusted and I'll have a look at what's here...'

Twisting a few dials and setting the magnification values to the correct scale, Dr Lilac took off his spectacles, placed them onto the table and then leaned in and hovered his eye over the viewing lens.

'Unbelievable...'

Andrew's grin grew wider.

'Oh dear me, is that the sound of somebody losing a bet?'

'Andrew, Mr Adams, I can see cells here, they're definitely alive and the way that they're moving, grouping together and then dividing, I know what this thing is doing. It's trying to regrow lost tissue.'

'Remarkable, isn't it?'

'I don't know what to think about it... I can't deny what I'm seeing, this... "thing" that you extracted from the tunnels, there are animals in nature that do this, salamanders and the like, but this... It's going too fast, nothing is able to perform cellular mitosis this quickly...'

Harvey stepped back from the table and adjusted his glasses.

'Something like this shouldn't be able to survive in these conditions, but it just does, and taken from something which had obviously been dead for an indeterminate amount of time... I don't understand...'

Andrew took a quick look through the microscope and confirmed what Harvey had seen, as Maxwell returned with a tray holding three coffees and sachets of sugar.

'So the biology of it is pretty unique for the kind of creature that it came from. We spent all of last year getting as much data as we could from it, well... Not me specifically, but there is only so much that the science team can do without a true expert on the job. So, Mr Voe, I would like to propose your full aid this time in furthering our understanding of what we can really do with what we've found here.'

Andrew nodded.

'It would be my pleasure. I have already come all this way so I don't see why not. What about you, Harvey?'

Harvey sighed but offered a handshake to show his acceptance.

'Well, you got me on this one. I'd say that even if I wasn't interested now, I still owe it to you.'

Maxwell backed away from them slightly and then straightened his posture, folding his arms in front of him.

'Mr Voe, you already knew much about the creature before arriving here so I'm aware that you know about the tests that we have conducted, exposing the specimen to different organisms?'

'Quite. From what looked to be a mutation in its ability to self-repair tissue there was another function that the cells were undertaking. When introduced to foreign tissue the specimen's cells remained separate. However when prompted by an external stimulus, in this instance being a small electrical charge, they reacted by essentially merging into them and creating whole new cells.'

Harvey squinted at Andrew briefly.

'Was that what you meant by "compatibility"? It assimilated them?'

'More like it fused with them. The new cells are a completely different entity,' Andrew explained, meshing his fingers together.

'Well, I should ask now, knowing that the subject is bound to be brought up sooner or later... What would your stance happen to be on human testing?'

Harvey paused with his coffee cup halfway to his lips. Andrew seemed oblivious.

'I would say it has its place in clinical drug trials; the world has a lot to benefit from the advancements that have been made as a result of it, Why? Were you thinking that we could splice the subject here into people or something?' Andrew said jokingly.

By this point, Harvey was gradually lowering his cup onto the table, beads of sweat starting to emerge on his forehead.

'Well, it certainly looks like you're on the ball today, Mr Voe.'

'I am? Wait… You're serious?'

'More than serious. Two successful trials and counting. In fact, that sample right there is taken from one of them.'

Without a word, Dr Lilac got up from his seat, spilling his drink in the process, then scrambling for the door, he threw it open and dashed outside while the other two looked on in shock. As Andrew got up to go after him, Maxwell gestured for him to stay.

'It's okay, I'm sure he will come to his senses sooner or later, I mean what does he really think he's going to do? Run outside and freeze?'

Andrew's gaze returned to the investor suddenly, with a determined look on his face.

'Now listen here, I'm sorry about my associate storming out like that but don't you think it would have been of the utmost importance to let me know via an e-mail at the very least if you were going to start this kind of testing? What kind of crazy town have I entered where a couple of positive lab results means you have the go-ahead to start sticking a bunch of needles in people? The side effects could be catastrophic!'

All of the humor and jovial demeanor was gone, replaced by an atmosphere that could only be considered dark. Now the investor seemed to tower over the young researcher who was starting to feel very alone in the room with him.

'Mr Voe. I believe it would be the couple of positive lab results that would give me unkillable soldiers who can just grow back an arm or a leg if it gets blown off and keep going, the kind that nobody in the world knows about, and the kind that I have complete control over because I own the whole damn thing' Maxwell casually explained, causing the remaining doctor to cower in his chair.

'How... How many tests have been made?'

'Oh, I don't know, twenty or so...' Maxwell ambled nonchalantly.

'And the... unsuccessful... trials?'

'They're not alive anymore if that's what you're asking. A pretty nasty way to go too. Hell, even the successful results had some rather unappealing side-effects, which is the whole reason why I invited you here in the first place. I want you to change up the formula so the results are more stable, less deaths, easier application'

Andrew withdrew, saying nothing.

'I'm not going to ask you nicely, we don't have to be friends for me to get what I want out of you and as for the good Doctor Lilac, I believe you have all of his research on file, is that right?'

Andrew nodded, not daring to step out of line.

'Excellent news. Then we will be packing up here during the next few months, seeing as I don't care much for the cold, and we'll be taking our little science project back home to Britain. I'm not going to chance it with you just yet, but as for Mr Lilac, I'm afraid that he will soon be finding himself much more "committed" to our work here than he was first led to believe.'

The investor then leaned over Andrew, his shadow completely eclipsing the terrified man and nudged his paper cup against Andrew's.

'Here's to making history, and to history being written by the winners.'

Pulling back from the busy rooms lined with scientists and workers, past a hole in the ground and a relic which rested lifelessly in its liquid chamber, and out of the shuttered doors, the round, metal dome of the research facility slowly sunk out of view, disappearing once more into the cold, blank ice and howling winds, as silently, history began to write itself where eyes could not follow...

CHAPTER TWO

I t was a rare occurrence to make a true friend within one of the bleak warehouses of Silverfish Packing Co., mainly due to their bizarre policies which had the factory-floor workers running around and swapping jobs like a bunch of crazed ants. It was a place where camaraderie went to die, at least that was the impression made on the workers who toiled on the lower end of the hierarchy.

Finn Lacksley, age 25, didn't have a single friend to his name and had been working in warehouse 12 for nearly three and a half years. In that time, he had seen management swap hands more than a dozen times, and floor staff come and go like traffic on the M3. Perhaps the most bugging thing about his co-workers was how they always ended up finding a new place to hide something that he was looking for and then vanish without a trace, and all before he had a chance to pull their ear about it. So it was on this day that Finn had to make another trek halfway across the factory and navigate through its labyrinth of walls, shelves, forklifts and pallet loaders to get a missing tool from his absent work partner, and more importantly, to bring him back to his workstation for the last job of the day.

His managers weren't the kind that cared very much if equipment got lost or "borrowed" which could set you back up to a few hours on getting a delivery ready, although they'd still have anyone who they saw as responsible shipped off to one of the more menial departments to rot. People who were employed just to move things around and tick boxes off checklists weren't exactly in high demand. It was a mercy then, that Finn took his job with utmost seriousness, and was prepared to cover for someone who wasn't pulling their weight, if only to ensure that he stayed in one place within the industry, putting what little pride he had in being able to get the job done and hand in his assignments on time. That being said, he had a tendency to keep to himself, not causing any kind of fuss and doing what he was told, which had the tried and tested effect of ensuring that the higher-ups ignored him and he could coast along in life without having to worry about changing his routine.

Right now, though, this was one of those times that disrupted that routine and got him in the mood for giving someone a harsh telling off. Being lumped with a new trainee who borrows his tools without letting him know and then goes off for lunch was one thing, but he had been gone for half an hour, and that was too far over Finn's limit when it came to letting work partners take extended breaks. There was only so far that he was willing to go before someone would get on his nerves, after all.

When Finn stepped out through one of warehouse 12's dull and dusty hallways, and out into the late evening air, he scanned around the poorly lit and scrap-cluttered loading bay to the shaded corner of the staff canteen. Between the steel shutters of the factory's truck bay and the barbed-wire garnished brick walls which separated the factory grounds from the road outside, there was a horrible little rectangular mobile-building nestled into one corner of the bay with unpleasant streaks of green mildew running down the sides of the faded outer walls. It wasn't hard to tell that the place had suffered water damage more than a few times, and the fridge inside was essentially a Pandora's box, reeking of things which had long since expired, but at least it had a nice clean microwave, if only because Finn was the one who cleaned it. That being said, it was more of a shed for having lunch in than a proper canteen, and most of the people in the warehouse preferred to bring a packed lunch and eat in one of the alcoves outside of the main building instead. The lights were on inside the canteen and Finn knew that would mean he was still in there, with any luck.

The trainee had only started his job here the day before yesterday and didn't know anybody else yet. Being the more experienced worker gave Finn a responsibility to look after his partner in his first week, for his own image more than anything else. After that he would have to seriously knuckle down if he wanted to meet Finn's standards and work with him on a regular basis; although he didn't seem to mind that not many workers would last that long, regardless. Back to reality, Finn approached the door from the outside, and with a deep breath, he put on a serious face, pushed it open and stepped in. Finn's colleague didn't seem to notice him right away as his back was turned to him, while he was sat down at a table on the far side of the canteen, but when he heard the flimsy door to the canteen slap against the wall, he snapped to attention.

'Come on Eric, you only get fifteen minutes to have lunch! You don't want to get in trouble with the guys upstairs do you?'

'Damnit… I'm sorry, Finn. I was looking through these boards that I think somebody lost and I completely zoned out, I should have come back and told you.'

Eric held up one of the four grimy clipboards that he had stacked in front of him, the first few pages were flipped through to one showing an order for some strange piece of medical equipment. The picture showed it as a kind of canister with a number of glass containers holding colored liquid which neither of them could identify, while in another document there was a picture of an assembly of robotic arms that looked like they were designed for holding something in place. Finn's expression cooled down a bit, but was still laced with suspicion when he took the clipboard from Eric and glanced down the page to see the reference time logged in from sometime last month. When he was done, Finn put the clipboard back in with the rest and focused his attention back on Eric, who was looking a bit nervous.

'I don't really want to think about what one of those is used for… That picture kind of makes my skin crawl.'

Finn thought he was probably just a bit squeamish about this kind of work.

'Look Eric, Silverfish ships all kinds of junk to clients. Nobody here actually has to test this stuff on site – that all gets handled client side'

Eric was still looking worried about it; Finn hadn't really thought that he would turn out to be the kind of guy who would brood over something like this at first… But the more he got to know the guy, the more his personality showed how he felt about things. That first-day facade of confidence was starting to wear off after this time and a couple of other panicky moments, trying and nearly failing to put things in the right place before Finn had to correct him. It made sense that he would have some irrational fears. Eric Jones was a bit of a lanky 19-year-old and looked like this was probably his first job too, fresh out of college and with nothing but hopeful expectations to show for it. Finn's patience was wearing thin.

'Okay mate, if this is going to bother you, I'll take these papers home and I'll sort it out, if that's what it takes for you to stop sulking. Now will you come back to the workstation? I want to get done on time.'

Eric perked up slightly, but it showed in his face that Finn had intimidated him.

'Yes Sir… I'm really sorry that I overreacted about this… And don't worry, I'll make up for the lost time right away!'

'And you don't have to call me "Sir", I'm not your boss.'

'Uh… Okay, Finn… I'm sorry…' Eric's voice trailed off.

With that, Finn took the papers from the clipboards and the tape measure back from Eric. It turned out he had just forgotten about it. Then both of them exited the canteen and headed back towards the factory, thankfully avoiding the rain which was just starting to pick up, and on the way back they chatted with each other about the rest of the work Eric would be doing in the factory, before they both got back to their corner of their workstation and started the finishing touches on their last order for the day.

Finn was going to have Eric carry the last package out towards the delivery truck as a mild punishment for making him wait to get it done, but seeing that he was struggling to carry it on his own, he decided to take some pity and hold one end while they moved it down the loading bay towards the delivery truck. On the way there, Finn noticed that Eric was unusually quiet compared to when they had been working on the last package.

'Are you still upset about those reference papers you found?' he enquired from his end of the box.

'Yeah… It's just the needles and scalpels and things like that. I just hate everything about them in general.'

Finn huffed, sounding his disapproval.

'Well, I don't suppose we will be dealing with this stuff anytime soon, unless we're swapping to a completely different set of clients from our usual lot, but I doubt it. Nobody has told me anything about that happening. Anyway, where was it that you found those clipboards?'

'They were jammed behind some cabinets in the hallway next to the locker room. They were stuck pretty far back as well. I had to get a crowbar just to lever them out.'

'Seriously, Eric? You need to let me know before doing that. The managers really don't like us moving equipment around without telling them and anything you do behind my back is liable to get me—'

'Oi! Watch where you're going!'

Neither Finn nor Eric had noticed that they nearly walked into one of the delivery-bay staff, who was now throwing a tantrum at them after having to suddenly dodge the pair. Eric, having been caught off guard, lost his grip on his end of the package and it was only saved from being broken by Finn, quickly hefting his side to lessen the fall, straining his arms somewhat as he did so. Quickly, they got the package back up and then hurried on towards the truck bay to drop it off next to a pile of neatly-stacked boxes, which were being checked over by another vested worker. When the delivery inspector was satisfied with the job, despite the scuffs, and ticked off the boxes for clearance on Finn's clipboard, both Finn and his partner headed back down the hallway towards the locker room to pack up, clock out and leave for the day.

'Alright Eric,' Finn sneered. 'I'm going to sort out this rubbish that you keep getting worked up about. You just go home and forget about it.'

Taking his hard hat off and hanging it up with the others, he dismissed Eric and picked up the papers again, musing that it probably wouldn't be too far a stretch to find out what kind of mad science rubbish the things in those order forms were. It would keep Eric a bit happier, at least up to the point when he would leave his area and not have to worry about working with him anymore, so he took them into one of the changing cubicles and shone a light on it from his phone to get a better look at it.

The document that Finn was reading wasn't the easiest piece of literature to decipher, some words and descriptions were covered up by blotches of dirt, grease or smudged ink, but the picture of it was mostly intact. One of them looked like something he would have expected to see in an operating theatre, either this was going to be delivered to some state-of-the-art medical facility, or someone out there was trying to build Dr. Frankenstein's evil lair. It was becoming apparent that a lot of the details on the paper just weren't adding up. Aside from the company logo, it was starting to look like these documents weren't even related to the warehouse at all. Finn checked the dates on the papers again which checked out the same time as when he saw it earlier on in the day: the third of May, 2:26am, which was dodgy in itself. Nobody worked in the factory that early on a Sunday.

Maybe the department handling it has something to do with it.

Finn had a look through the papers trying to find a clue to which department would be handling it, and was even more intrigued to find that not only was there no mention of who would be handling and shipping it off, but also that the contractor's name, all contact details, and every one of the check boxes that the inspectors were meant to sign were absent; only the time of arrival and the bay number for the truck were still there at the bottom of the page. Flicking the paper over to try and see if it was a double-sided print, Finn had to stifle a wheezing laugh over what he saw next. There was what looked like a hastily scrawled note on the back of the page which read out in big, scratchy letters: BEWARE! SKULKERS!

Alright, not what I expected. If they're calling us lazy then they had better beware indeed, lest they run into me on a bad day.

Obviously this was a joke now. Somebody had been down to the printers and edited in a bunch of documents to make them look like something out of a science fiction film, and then stuffed them somewhere that they thought would be hard to find, so that the next guy who had to clean the place would find them, think there's a conspiracy going on, and then probably arrive to work the next day with a tinfoil hat. Elaborate, but effective. Finn would have to give them style points for that. As for Eric, he would break the news to him that they weren't real and to stop being such a cry-baby about it. Finn was sure that there was probably many more "hilarious" mind games in the documents, and he would have more than enough time to pick them out during his days off. That's if he still cared about it at that point. With that, Finn flicked off the light on his phone and changed into his home clothes, then stuffed the papers into his bag and working overalls up on the rack, clocked out at the card reader by the side-entrance, then almost immediately regretted walking outside. Still in a daze from earlier, the door automatically closed and locked itself behind him, leaving him running through the wind and rain to get to his car.

After getting into his car, throwing his already damp rucksack into the back seat as quickly as humanly possible and then starting the engine, he was in the process of getting comfortable in the driver's seat when he noticed, looking through the rain-covered windshield, that Eric was still waiting with a couple of other employees under the bus stop, just down the road from the warehouse. The factory was a fair distance away from the rest of civilization, out in the countryside and surrounded by trees, it was a wonder that the place had as many staff as it did, and as such, waiting times for buses were sometimes long and infrequent.

He wasn't talking to anyone else while sat at the station and was just staring down the road, occasionally checking the time on his phone.

Well, have fun getting home, you little hindrance, Finn thought, callously.

He then flicked on his headlights, the heaters, and the car radio, and finally pulled out of the factory's car park, heading towards home.

CHAPTER THREE

The rain continued to pour, collecting in deep puddles which ran up and down the lonely street, and pattered furiously on the roof of the bus shelter and the forest's canopy opposite Eric's place of work. Thankfully for him, it was drowning out most of the chatter from the other workers waiting at the bus stop and letting him get a little more peace for himself, something that he needed after today. He raised his head from the glow of his phone screen and stood up from the bus stop's bench, when the sound of an approaching bus and the ghostly beams of its front headlights broke through the dark, wet night. He stepped out from underneath the shelter as it came to a halt, choosing to sit in a quiet spot further to the back end of the vehicle, despite the bus not being particularly crowded. Sitting around groups of people just wasn't his thing, and it's not like he really knew any of them very well anyway.

It surprised Eric that Finn had accepted to look into what he had found, especially after all of the mishaps that he had made while on his training schedule so far, which had given him such a clumsy impression. Rooting around in his hoodie's pocket for a moment, he took his phone back out and pressed the power.

9:36PM - Weather / Stormy.

Eric saw the display and yawned, slipping the phone into his jeans.

Yeah, no kidding it's stormy... And if I had to wait half an hour for this bus to arrive, then I must have just missed the last one by a hair.

Eric hadn't run particularly fast to get to the bus stop and the dark green hoodie that he wore over his shirt was feeling a bit damp. Sighing, he took the sweatshirt off and wrapped the sleeves around his waist, which wasn't an amazingly comfortable thing to do while sitting down in a moving vehicle.

I can't believe what a fool I've been today, wasting time with those files, dropping that package, not reading the weather forecast and bringing my waterproof coat... What a mess... I can't wait to be back home and get some rest...

Piling on to Eric's sullen demeanor, he felt a rumble emanate from his stomach.

...And get something to eat because I'm stupid and didn't have lunch on my break.

For the rest of the way home, Eric folded his arms on the back of the seat in front of him and buried his head in them, half dozing off, but still listening to the monotonous voice of the automated stop announcer which blared over the rumble of the engine until it announced his stop, at which point he threw his rucksack back over his shoulders and made his way down the bus to the door outside, and stepped out onto the edge of a series of residential districts.

This time, Eric made sure to run. The cold, wet weather belted down on him, absolutely drenching him from head to toe. He even took a wrong step at one point and ended up treading into a much deeper puddle than he had first anticipated, getting water all inside his shoe. Only another block down and he would be home, to get out of his wet apparel, take a quick shower and collapse on his bed, ready for a good night's sleep. The sodden shoe squelched horribly with each step and brought about the unpleasant feeling of the rainwater seeping into his sock. He almost wished that it was both shoes just so it was consistent, but pushed away the thought and carried on, sweeping past rows of flats, many still lit and glowing with the orange light of late-evening life. The worst of it was feeling how cold his arms and fingers were getting without any kind of protection, and he shivered, hoping that he didn't catch a cold outside. Upon getting within running distance of his front door, a self-trained instinct kicked in, where he unconsciously reached into his pocket to grasp for his keys and he pulled them free without much hassle, making getting inside all the easier.

Upon getting through his front door and into the well-lit coat hall of his home, Eric briefly basked in the warmth emanating from the radiator which was situated directly under a line of coat hooks to the right of the front entrance. Eric's parents were a considerate couple and had left the lights and heating on for him, knowing that he would be coming home after they went to bed. Through an archway and into the living room there was a short table, a pair of settees and an average-sized flat screen television which was switched onto a dead channel and displaying a solid blue color which illuminated the room. Eric made his way over to it and pressed a button on the side, switching it off.

Feeling hungry and tired, Eric made his way through the living room and into the kitchen where he opened up the fridge to take out two slices of bread and slot them into the toaster, also taking out the margarine and a jar of peanut butter. It wouldn't be a full dinner but right now that didn't matter; just getting something to eat was the priority. He stepped out of the kitchen briefly to deposit his soaked hoodie into the wash basket in the laundry closet, when he jumped at the creaking sounds of footsteps coming down from the stairwell.

Damn, had I really been that loud? Oh well, I guess I have to deal with this now...

'Eric? Is that you, home?' came a man's voice from the living room. He was speaking in a restrained voice and moving closer to the kitchen, where Eric had just been.

'Yeah, Dad, it's me.'

'Just a little quieter please, everyone else is still sleeping. I heard you come in.'

Eric lowered his voice with his next reply.

'Okay. Thanks for leaving the lights on for me.'

Glancing over his shoulder, Eric could see that his father had now entered the kitchen, wearing a nightgown and rubbing the sleep from his eyes. His father made his way over to the kitchen cupboard and picked out a glass to take over to the sink and filled it with water.

'You must have been soaked getting home, I noticed that you didn't take your coat with you.'

'Yeah, it's pretty horrid out today, I really should have planned ahead for it but seeing as the last few days were fairly sunny, I thought I could just chance it and wear a sweatshirt.'

'Good news then that we've just pulled some fresh towels out of the dryer. On a side note, you're making toast?' Eric's father queried, pointing at his plate.

Eric shut the lid of the wash basket and looked up at his Dad glumly.

'I kind of forgot to have lunch today, just a lot of things on my mind at the moment, is all.'

Taking a sip of water and responding with a stern look, Eric's father stepped over to him and responded.

'They're treating you alright in there aren't they? They're not making you skip lunch to get more work done while they laze off, I hope?'

'Oh no, it's nothing like that, I was just forgetful. I've been getting on really well with the guy they paired me up with and he's patient with me.'

Eric's father smiled warmly.

'That's good to hear. I just came down for some water and to see how you were. You have a good night and I'll see you in the morning.'

'Thanks Dad, see you in the morning.'

With that, Eric's dad took the rest of his water and went back out of the room and up the stairs, leaving Eric once more alone in the kitchen.

A metallic ping sounded that the toast was done, so Eric gingerly pinched at the corners of each slice dragging them out and onto a plate. He then spread on the margarine and peanut butter onto both slices and ate them on a wooden chair just outside of the laundry closet. Nearby, there was a window overlooking the back garden which was pitch black and pouring with rain.

Well… not really patient with me. More, kind of condescending, like he didn't really want to work with me and was just putting up with me because he had to… But I'm not gonna tell Dad that. He doesn't need to have another thing to worry about… Not after the last time…

Eric put his empty plate down on the windowsill and looked at his left hand, it was missing a third and fourth finger, and he remembered back to when it had happened...

...At the time, Eric had been hopeful, full of energy, and with a passion to match his ambition to score a job that both himself and his family could be proud of. Finishing secondary school and brimming with confidence, he set about studying a number of courses at his local college, opting for ones that would allow him to work with his hands and really put his creativity to good use. He had chosen carpentry as one of these courses. Perhaps it could have been something that developed into a career in that field, but alas, it was not meant to be. This was all thanks to a poorly secured pressing machine, a new device which had been installed as an upgrade from the faculty's outdated predecessor. The machine was a bulky and obtuse device, and it weighed like an anvil. It certainly felt like an anvil when it dropped a couple of inches and closed the gap between the stand that it should have rested on without any faults, and the table beneath it. A gap where Eric's hand had been resting while he was using it to finalize one of his last projects.

Crunch

The next few moments were filled by a blistering agony which engulfed his entire hand. While he was yelling out in pain, the rest of the class were screaming and panicking, and the instructors were desperately trying to calm everybody down. In the chaos, Eric had done the one thing that would keep him up at night regretting. Thinking that he needed to free himself, he pulled on his hand, hard. It was a stupid decision and had resulted in what he would describe as perhaps the worst pain in his life. The fingers that were stuck tore off at the knuckle and he was left with two aching stumps, trailing ripped skin and gushing blood. A couple of the other students fainted and he had to be taken to the hospital that day, but it couldn't hold a candle to the disappointment that he felt weeks later, knowing that the incident would scare him into dropping the course...

It was a miracle that he had been accepted for this job. Having less strength to grip things and carry them meant that he was having to rely on his partner a lot more than he wanted to. It made him feel like a burden and that he wasn't wanted, and when he could hear his partner muttering under his breath, just how much he was slowing him down; it made him feel truly awful.

Thankfully Eric's phone hadn't got wet while he was out in the rain, and he took it out and rested it on the kitchen counter while taking off the rest of his wet clothes to put away, he then put his plate away in the dishwasher and took the phone up with him to his room where he dried off with one of the towels his Dad had mentioned and slipped under the covers of his bed, leaving the phone charging at a port near his bedside chest of drawers.

In the middle of the night, sometime after 1:00 a.m., Eric's phone buzzed a few times, but was unable to wake him from his deep sleep, and he continued to doze off into the night.

CHAPTER FOUR

*W*hat the bleeding hell do you mean "not suitable material for workplace discussion"?

Finn had planned on posting the pictures of those clipboards that somebody had hid away in the warehouse as a practical joke, up on the warehouse's unofficial forum, a phone app that he had been encouraged to join when he had first signed up three years ago, and the pictures were almost immediately taken down by an anonymous administrator in the group, and issued him a warning as well as a block to all his chat activities, that included the notice board where he could find his working hours, which was currently what was making Finn so angry.

I mean, who does this numbskull even think he is?! Somebody was posting a video of his effing cat falling off an armrest not three days ago and I can't show them something even if it's relevant?

Finn took a draw from his cigarette and puffed a cone of smoke out of the open window that he was leaning over.

Oh, and their timing was impeccable – bloody "fun-police" must have been up all hours of the night just to catch that one out, not that there should have been any problem with it at all. Now, that must mean that either one of them just has some kind of idiotic vendetta against me or that this admin is in on the joke and he's covering for his friends. Well, if that's the case, I'll bite and take them in on my next day at work, see what the offices make of them, hopefully I can find the guy there and get him to unblock me too, seeing as he's not responding to my messages all of a sudden.

Frustrated, Finn flicked the stub of his cigarette out into the rain, closed the window and turned around a bit too fast, and bumped his side into the pool table that took up nearly three quarters of his entrance room.

Bloody stupid thing! I should have got rid of this years ago.

Finn huffed and awkwardly shimmied past the obstruction, before his traipse took him into the room where he slept; not really a proper bedroom because it was also the place where he did his cooking and got ready in the morning, but first-time home buying hadn't left him with an excess of space to put his belongings or a wealth of choice when it came to what those belongings would be. That, and a combination of poor decisions and general laziness, had led to him cutting corners when it came to living arrangements, like for instance, the pool table in the other room. That was a mistake which he had bought when he was younger and never sold off, mainly because he didn't like the thought of having to go through the hassle of putting it up for sale and dragging it out to the road where he could load it into someone else's car.

Switching on the lights, he found the room to be perfectly how he left it: a mess. Most of the walls had posters pinned up onto them from various metal bands, a good portion of the floor was covered in discarded clothes, and his mattress which lay on the floor with a duvet half-covering it had a stain from where he had spilt coffee onto it from tripping over in the morning during breakfast.

It is way too late to be dealing with this rubbish... I'll just sleep on the side that isn't wet and I can worry about cleaning it in the morning, Finn thought drearily while stumbling over to his bed.

He was just about to settle down when his phone buzzed, sounding an alert to him. Irritated, he flipped over the duvet and unlocked it.

Well, isn't this rich, the "fun-policeman" himself finally decides to reply to my messages. Let's see what he's got to say for himself.

Finn scrolled down the page which listed a couple of paragraphs' worth of text and went through cycles of being annoyed and confused as he read it.

"Don't reply to this message, you're still blocked, delete the pictures and don't tell anybody else about this, you are in terrible danger."

What is this guy on? And he wants me to be back into work asap to deliver the documents to him? I knew it, he's in on this. I'll show up with the documents in hand, waltz on into the office and they'll all be waiting to throw a pie in my face, my bet. Damn him for holding my account hostage for it though, I'm just going to have to grin and bear it until I can get it back. Hopefully HR catches wind of it and gets them sacked for this. That's if they're not in on it too.

Finn flicked the power off on his phone, folded the covers over himself and desperately tried to get in the mood to drift off, but found himself distracted by the thought of having to confront the people whose joke he had fallen for at work on his next day in, coupled with the damp patch of coffee on his duvet, which was further over than he had first anticipated and starting to stick on his arm. Frustrated by both of these things, Finn unwrapped himself from his duvet and bundled it up so that it would fit in the washing machine easier.

Absolutely useless this is. If I'm too pissed off to get any sleep right now, then I'll just have to put it on to wash and find something else to sleep under. I think there's a clean sheet in a cupboard somewhere around here...

Upon opening up his washing machine, stuffing the duvet into it and reaching inside to insert a detergent pod, Finn was startled by the sounds of shouting coming from outside, and in a panic, hit his head on the rim while trying to take his head out.

'Ack! What the fuck is going on?!!' Finn exclaimed to the world in general, losing his temper.

Finn got up from his crouching position and angrily pulled back the curtain on his window, just enough to stick his head through and see what was going on. What happened next was a blur of events. From behind the window Finn could see out onto the street from his first-floor apartment and onto the road below, where the orange glow of streetlights illuminated a somewhat flooded road under them. A large white van was parked behind some bushes and a tree, on the edge of the road, where an expansive forest stretched out behind it. The van was very difficult to make out in the rain and because of how it was partially obscured by foliage, but the rain had died down enough that it was visible from Finn's perspective. Both back doors were wide open on the van.

Trying to get a better look by pressing closer to the glass window, Finn saw that one of the back doors was shaking slightly and there was a pair of hands grasping the end of the door, a left hand and a right hand, one above the other, like there was someone hanging on and trying not to be pulled in. After a second or two of continued shouting, a figure clad in black clothing came around the left side of the vehicle and pried the hands off of the van's door, and then entered into the back. At the front of the vehicle, the headlights came on and the van began to move off, doors still open at first but closing as it turned off into the forest and disappeared from view.

'Bloody hell… What was that all about?' Finn whispered to himself.

He backed away from the curtains and cast a glance towards his phone, which lay on the floor, on top of a small pile of clothes beside his mattress. Finn's thoughts became immediately wracked with questions, doubts and fears, swirling around in his head as he searched for a decision.

It is exactly this kind of madness that makes me paranoid… Did I just see somebody getting kidnapped? What the hell was he doing, stuffing somebody into a van at gone past midnight? Was that even what happened? And did anybody else see it? Do I call the police?

Finn groaned and cupped is face into his palms.

For. Pete's. Sake. It is too late for this. I have to stop worrying about every little thing that goes on and just focus on what matters, what just happened outside could have been seen by anyone else in my apartment block, and is, henceforth, not my problem. Get a sheet out of the cupboard, get into bed and get some rest, Finn, you paranoid git.

After slapping some sense into himself, Finn decided he'd had enough for the night and got the sheet out of his cupboard, before getting in and doing everything he could to push back the dark cloud of worry that was filling up his mind, and after a good few minutes of trying, he succeeded in forcing his way into a deep, dreamless sleep.

Meanwhile inside a van, trundling through the forest in the midst of the damp and pitch-black night…

'Let me go, damnit! I don't know any of you! I don't know what you want! just let me go!'

A middle-aged man, bearded and dressed in a foul-smelling, worn-out coat, kicked and shouted as three hooded figures, all with faces masked by bandanas, wrestled to restrain him in the dark. All of them were unable to see but perfectly able to hear and feel the struggle that was going on.

'God damnit! Will one of you just flick on a torch already? I can't do anything if I can't see a damn thing!'

'Well, I don't have one. I thought you're the one who had it!'

'I left mine in the front seat when you started dragging him in! Just one of you-'

A series of bangs came from the front of the van, and a slot opened up in the divider between the front section and the back, where another masked man from the second passenger seat shone a light through the slot and onto a scene of three men trying to hold another one down, who was still shouting and pleading.

'Do I have to spell it out for you, knuckleheads!? Put him out already!'

One of the masked assailants glanced back and complained.

'Yeah, easier said than done, just hold the damn light steady!'

The one making the complaint returned and leaned in next to the associate closest to him.

'Alright, we're going to swap. When we do, I'll get in under his neck and choke him out, you just hold him still. Ready? One, two...'

In a split second, the second assailant grabbed onto the arm which was let go of by the first, and the first assailant swiftly locked his arm under the throat of the man who they were all pinning down. The man spluttered, desperately trying to kick off his attackers and wasting his energy, with three men on top of him. His strength failing, the man eventually passed out and slumped onto the floor of the van.

Sarcastic clapping could be heard coming from the front seat as each of the assailants breathed heavily in regaining their stamina.

'Oh, shut your face! Us back here did a fine job with finding the guy, not that you were any help.'

'Oh what? You mean the fine job you did nearly waking up the whole neighborhood bringing him back after you found him? Yeah, great job! You should really give yourselves a pat on the back!'

As one of the conscious men in the back got up and rushed towards the divider, the one in the front seat quickly closed it and left them all in complete darkness again.

'Bellend!'

'Well, it's no use calling him that now. Just sit back and enjoy the ride, we'll be at the factory before morning to drop off the drunk, and that'll be job done.'

The one who responded sat down against the van's inner wall and tried to get comfortable, as the van continued to rock and bounce at every muddy ridge and tree root that it passed over.

'Yeah, I should hope we'll be back before morning. I despise getting on this job, going to these backwater places to snatch boozers off the street and bring them back, smelling of piss and spirits. When are we actually going to start taking people who matter?'

A third voice from the back of the van chimed in, deeper than the others but just as muffled by his face mask, sounding stern and with an air of authority.

'When the client wants us to grab people who matter. The whole reason why we're taking people who don't, is because nobody asks questions about it. Is that too difficult for you to understand?'

The two other figures stared in the general direction of the third voice.

'Well, excuse me for having aspirations. Not like we haven't been doing this for a few years now and might just want a higher rate of pay at some point. Something to give us a reason to celebrate after—'

It seemed that this wasn't an acceptable response, as the third voice applied a more serious tone.

'Let me make this perfectly clear in case you forgot. You're not here because we're one big happy team, who do our jobs because we're best friends. You, me and the rest of us here are dead men if the client says he's done with us. He will send his goons to find us in the night and take us away if we so much as think about stepping out of line, so if you want to be the one who's hankering for a nice ol' chat with this lunatic about maybe getting a fatter pay cheque at the end of the month, be my guest, but don't be surprised if he invites you downstairs and we never see you again.'

The other two looked to the floor where the drunk lay softly breathing and contemplated.

'Just had to kill the mood, didn't you?'

Outside of the van the pillars of trees loomed past as the van drove on between them, winding and weaving as it changed its course and continued on, as the rain beat down on it.

CHAPTER FIVE

Monday. Finn's hand twitched, holding a teaspoon in one hand and rubbing the sand from his eyes with the other. They were a little bloodshot, as evidenced by his lack of sleep over the weekend. Half-dressed and not-at-all feeling ready for work, Finn yawned, open mouthed, and stared down into his mug.

Why is it so damned difficult to keep the promises I make to myself?

Hearing the kettle come to a boil and finish with an audible click, he glanced over to it absent-mindedly, and tipped his heaped teaspoon of sugar without looking. When he remembered what he was doing and looked back, he saw that he had missed the mug by millimeters and dumped the whole spoonful onto the counter.

Load of rubbish... This, and this whole weekend.

With an annoyed grumble, Finn lifted the mug, held it under the counter, and then cupped a hand over the spilled sugar, herding it into the mug, where it showered over a bed of instant coffee grind at the mug's base.

I tell myself; "Everything's going to be alright Finn! The documents, the white van men, the state of the garbage heap that you're living in, everything is going to be A-Okay!"

Finn reached over and lifted up the kettle to pour some boiling water into his mug.

Of course, saying that only makes me worry even more, then it gets to the point where I'm stressing myself out over this so much that it all just boils over and I end up being constantly miffed about everything, and unable to get anything done! I don't want to feel like this, it shouldn't be my problem!

The kettle thumped back down onto its rest, despite Finn trying not to slam it.

This is just me, being delusional... I need to take more responsibility. I have priorities today; get the documents handed in to get my phone app's block lifted; help poor, useless Eric with his training shift, and then go home and get this place cleaned up... Oh, and as for that van, I haven't seen it around since Friday night, so odds are that it either skipped town or they're being locked up as we speak, so that's one worry alleviated right away.

Last was the milk, poured in steadily and stirred, leaving him with the staple beverage of his morning routine, left for a minute or two to cool while he checked his phone, and then sipped down alongside a couple of dry biscuits. With breakfast over, Finn ambled through the rest of his morning preparations, getting dressed, packing lunch and the documents into his bag. Gradually the coffee was starting to kick in, and he felt more alert as a result. Out of the front door and standing straight with his worker's uniform on, bag slung over his shoulder and car keys in one hand, Finn feigned a cheery smile.

Today is going to be a good day. Keep believing it and it might just happen.

However, it wasn't a moment after completing that innocuous thought, that he was face to face with someone who had slipped his memory and was an unpleasant reminder of yet another priority – perhaps Finn's most urgent to consider.

'Ah, there's the man I need to see... So, where is it? Huh?' The man snidely began, as he closed the distance between them. He was quite portly, tattooed, and wore an ensemble that could be best described as "the full douchebag experience".

'Alright, you've got me, Steve. I'll have the rent paid in soon, I just need to sell some—'

'Furniture? Electronics? A bit of the old "magic powder"? Sell whatever you damn want, just get me my rent by next week. You don't want me and the lads to come around and spoil your evening, do you?' he threatened.

'No, seriously, I'll have the money for you soon, I swear,' Finn pleaded in defense.

'Good, so nice that you agree, now get lost!' The landlord spat and shoved Finn out of his way.

Christ... And another thing, pay the damned rent to this piece of human garbage...

Stepping off to the left and using stairwell to get the ground floor, he found himself having to squeeze past a couple of hooded loiterers on the way down.

'Excuse me.'

'Yeah, just keep walking, bozo. We're not here for you... Yet.'

Finn didn't look back at the remark, he just kept walking to his car out in the parking bay and got in, putting his work bag in the back seat and starting the engine.

I hope I don't find those rats still here when I get back, I swear it's just getting worse and worse around here all the time... In fact...

Looking in the wing mirror, Finn noticed that the two guys from the stairs were now joined by a third, and were circling around to the back end of the apartment block to go behind them.

Just what I thought, it makes sense that they were waiting for their dealer to arrive. If you want to waste your life shooting up drugs and waking up in a dumpster in the next town over, be my guest.

Putting the thought out of his mind, Finn turned off and onto the main road, where he followed it along until the memory of his route led him back to Silverfish Packing Co: Warehouse 12. His home away from home.

Moments after swiping his ID to get in through the staff entrance, Finn found himself being confronted by another worker, one from another department as evidenced by his office-worker-styled clothing, who was acting rather panicked when he noticed Finn arrive.

'Are you Finn Lacksley? Tell me it's you. I recognise your face from the profile picture.'

'Yeah, it's me, but slow down… What's this all about?' Finn replied.

The office worker pointed to Finn's bag.

'You've got them in there, right? The papers you stole. I need them right now!' He demanded.

Finn flinched at that accusation and replied with a concerned look.

'I've got the papers but I don't know what you mean by stolen. From what I heard they were just lying around, so don't go implying I'm a thief!'

Diving into Finn's bag, the man snatched the documents out with little regard for Finn's personal belongings, which spilled out as he scoured the bag for any and all traces of the papers.

'Hey, come on! I went to the effort of hanging on to these, the least you do is give a "Thanks".'

The worker seemed to be looking at Finn with a mix of anger and despair now.

'Who told you they were just lying around?'

'Alright, look here, I'm not looking for an argument today so could you just cool it down? I'll tell you what I know.'

This seemed to have a sobering effect on the distressed office worker, and he took a moment to regain his posture and straighten his tie.

'Okay? I'll start at the beginning. Last Friday I was on mentoring duty for a new general assistant, his name is Eric, he found the papers behind some cabinets and he was getting upset over them, so he gave them to me to try and find out who they belonged to. I looked, and didn't find any leads, but what I did find was a load of cheap Halloween gimmicks.'

The officer worker frowned.

'Halloween gimmicks? Like what?'

'Well, one of them had this spooky, cryptic message scribbled on the back – you can see it on the back of this page, here,' Finn explained.

Finn flipped through and showed him the note, still there, scratched onto the paper as clear as day: BEWARE! SKULKERS!

'Damn... Why like this? I-I'm not stopping to explain, I'm just going to take these and go!'

The office worker was visibly panicking now and was stuffing the papers into a leather briefcase which was slung under his shoulder.

'Jeez, man... Don't get started with this again, those papers are just an office prank, what's all the fuss about?'

'It's not a bloody joke to me! Just listen: I'm going to put these back where they belong. If you've still got pictures on your phone, delete them, for God's sake, and forget this ever happened. As for your friend, Eric, just tell him you lost the papers. We never met.'

And with that, the office worker hurried out of the room and around a corner.

What a freaking weirdo… I was just about to ask him about unbanning me on my phone and he just bolts off like that. He'd better do it later today or I'll be going into the office and having a word with him about it.

Out of his peripheral vision, Finn saw the door to the staff's entrance being opened, and he turned to see Eric stepping through, looking a little down.

'Oh, hey Eric, how've you been?' Finn asked in an insincerely cheerful tone.

'A bit run down… Caught a cold over the weekend. I was going to ask you over that phone thing, if you had any news on those documents I found last week, but I couldn't get through to you.'

'Oh yeah, the phone app. About that… I'm just going to get changed and I'll tell you all about it after we've got set up.'

Later that day, now in their corner of the warehouse, Finn piped up again while helping to seal packages for shipping. By this point, Finn had already filled his partner in on some of the details.

'So, all this happened because of the papers I found?' Eric said, feeling guilty.

'Well, I posted them, thinking that I could get some answers, and then somebody got mad about it for no discernible reason and bans me… Anyway, it's all done now, some raving lunatic from the office department came down and snatched them off my hands this morning.'

Eric peered over the stack of goods that he was working on to give Finn an inquisitive look.

'Are they usually like that?'

'What? Raving lunatics? I wouldn't know. Not really my department, but anyway, you just missed my chat with him when you came in, which is probably a good thing to be fair. He started interrogating me over it, and all the while he's acting like he owes the mafia money or something. Really sketchy behaviour.'

'Yikes… You're right, looks like I dodged a bullet there.'

'Well, less of a bullet and more just like an extra helping of icing on the crazy cake that's been building up this weekend. I still have pictures of the papers, some of which I don't know if you've seen yet. The fruit-case who I just met wanted me to delete them, but you know what? He can shove off. I'll keep them just to spite him.'

During their lunch break, Finn and Eric retreated to the privacy of the neglected canteen. While Finn was passing a shop-bought dinner through the microwave, he gave Eric his phone in order to see the pictures, who flicked from picture to picture, scanning them for anything out of place.

'Hey Finn, I really don't like the look of this…'

Finn tore off the film on his dinner which had just come out of the microwave and recoiled as a small cloud of hot steam was released. Looking at the picture Eric was showing from his phone, he saw that it was the one of the handwritten warning.

'Yep, that's the one that got him all worked up. I'd say it's a load of rubbish if you ask me.'

Eric swiped to the next picture and, finding that this was the case, replied: 'So what you're saying is: this was just here on the back of the page, and that crazy guy from the office department was trying to keep this from getting out by blocking you when you tried to upload it?'

'Something like that... Well, the guy who blocked me might not be him specifically, but it would make sense considering that he knew about it... Makes me wonder who else has been scheming around here.'

Eric placed Finn's phone down and folded his arms on the table in front of him, while Finn sat down next to him with his dinner and a plastic fork in hand.

'So... You've been working here for a lot longer than me, have you noticed anything suspicious like this happening before?'

Finn pondered this for a moment while prodding at the dry surface of his slightly overcooked microwave lasagne.

'It would not shock me if there was... I probably just haven't noticed because I haven't been paying enough attention.'

'I'm just asking because it seems to me like finding those documents, getting punished for posting pictures of them, and then having someone who is clearly not in their right mind as you put it, come down and demand that you hand them over is all connected, right?'

Finn chuckled through a mouthful of his dinner and then swallowed.

'That would be what they want you to think, wouldn't it?'

'You... Think they're doing this to wind us up?' Eric questioned.

'What a critical observation, Sherlock. My guess is that they'll do it to just about anyone who they happen to want to get a rise out of when they stumble along and take the bait. If you're not convinced and want to follow it up to see what kind of spectacular punchline lies at the end of this ongoing gag, don't say I didn't warn you'

Eric looked at Finn solemnly and sighed.

'Well, I guess I should thank you for the warning if that's the case. Anyway, I put my number on your phone so that I could send the pictures over in a text message. There's just one last thing that I want to check out, then I'll be done with this'

'Okay, so like I said, it's your call if you want to follow up on this stuff, just let me know if something bad happens, I'm not taking the blame if you get into trouble,' Finn reiterated before shoveling in another scoop of lasagne.

'Well… uh… I thought that I would do something for you as well, just as a thanks,' Eric said, before taking a small packet of mints out of his pocket and leaving them on the table beside Finn's meal.

Finn glanced down at them and raised an eyebrow, before swallowing and starting up again.

'You went out and bought me sweets? What made you think that I would want these?' Finn asked, pushing them away.

'Well, I just wanted to get along with people here, so I thought that if somebody does something good for me, I should do something for them to show that I'm grateful…'

Finn felt put on by this and felt a pang of pity for him.

'Honestly Eric, if you do that, all that's going to happen is people are going to start using it as an excuse to take advantage of you. Don't spend your money on people who aren't worth it,' Finn explained coldly, before finishing off the last of his food and getting up to leave.

'Could you humor me though? I know that I can be a pain sometimes, but I'd like to be able to make up for it, just a little bit…'

It was true, he had been putting up with him more than he usually did with other trainees. Maybe it was his injury that was making him feel guilty about being harsh on him. Their companionship was still something that he eventually wanted to put behind him however and deciding change his mind and take this small gift that Eric had provided wasn't going to change that. After the exchange, he left the canteen with the packet of mints stuffed into one of his pockets, and Eric tagging along behind him.

Within the corrugated steel walls of Warehouse 12, past the bustling factory floor and into the office block which dominated the back section of the building with its rows of isolating cubicles, one of these cubicles contained a pair of jittering hands, attempting to hold a landline telephone steady as their owner dialled through frayed nerves.

'Please, please, please, for the love of God, don't be mad...'

The dial tone of the landline phone rang, taking precious time in the minutes before an answer was passed through.

'Name and pass code?' came a calm voice from the other end.

The office worker scanned around his closed-off cubicle, making absolutely certain that nobody was listening in on his conversation.

'Josh Barnsley... Access code; three... two... three... one... seven.'

The phone went silent for a minute while the worker nervously waited, listening to the sounds of papers rustling over the other side.

'That checks out. What do you have to report, Mr Barnsley?'

The office worker took a deep breath, hesitated for a moment, and answered.

'There's been a-another hidden message. I think there is another mole trying to expose—'

'Has the matter been dealt with or is it ongoing?' the voice interrupted.

That last response from the person on the other side had been less mellow than his other replies, pressing a subtle authority onto the worker and adding to his distressed disposition.

'I-it has... been dealt with. I have the message right here along with all of the lost documents...'

'And nobody else saw them?'

'No... D-d-definitely not...' the office employee stuttered.

The next response was repeated in the same calm tone as before, but this time it was saturated in an undertone of menace.

'Mr Barnsley, it's a shame that you seem to think it is acceptable to lie to us...'

The office worker swallowed, tensing up as the words trickled out of the phone and rested their sinister weight on him.

'I have everything on your report here in front of me here: 36 years of age, married. I hear you're expecting a child soon. I wonder how that will turn out...'

The worker stopped dead, a cold dread had overwhelmed him.

'Two guys... Just two guys, nobodies... They didn't even know what they were, I swear.'

Another awful minute dragged on while the sounds of keyboard-tapping, printing and talking outside of the cubicle continued to contrast the growing grief that this worker was going through.

'Names?'

The office employee's eyes swivelled to meet the phone that he was holding up to his ear. Panic was now setting in.

'Please… you really don't have to do this. They really didn't know what it meant, they're clueless, honest!' he pleaded.

'Give us their names, Mr. Barnsley,' the voice replied, as if asking a child to behave.

The worker cowered over his table, giving up.

'Fi-Finn… Lacksley….'

'And the other?'

'Uh… It was someone called… Eric… I think?'

Again, the phone went silent, in the meantime the Josh searched around his office table and picked out a paper bag which was half filled with wrapped toffees and emptied them out neatly onto the table.

'Eric, hm… I'm not sure that we have a file on this Eric fellow yet. Must be new. Nevertheless, good job. On a side note, remember that you are due downstairs next Monday as per our "special employment arrangement". Have a pleasant evening Mr. Barnsley.'

The tone for the phone's disconnection sounded, and with a shaking hand, the office worker set the phone back down on its rest. When it was free, he raised the empty paper bag to his lips and hyperventilated into it until his nerves had settled.

'Oh God, forgive me… What have I done?'

CHAPTER SIX

Days passed, and with clearer skies, the mid-June heat began to pick up. The lingering moisture which had been present since last Friday's storm had dried up and the pavement outside baked under the midday sun. It was peak heatwave season.

Finn Lacksley entered his home through the front door after spending most of the day wandering around his local town square – going to various shops, having lunch at a cafe and making a quick stop at an arcade to see if it could cure his boredom. It didn't.

With the relaxing day that Finn had planned coming to a close, he returned home just as it was starting to get dark outside, carrying with him two full shopping bags containing everything from the dinners he would be eating over the course of the next week, to the six-pack of beers that he would be drinking at home on his own. Finn wasn't a particularly heavy drinker but always preferred to drink within the privacy of his apartment.

Why is it always at this time of year that the weather is either buckets of rain or boiling me alive? Make your damn mind up, England.

Finn covered his mouth to stifle a yawn and then dumped his shopping down by the door, locking it behind him. He then picked them back up again and into the living space, where he sifted through the plastic bags and sorted the contents into rows on his kitchen counter. When the contents were all neatly arranged, he began to put them away in their respective places, but paused for a moment to look at the cover of a free magazine which he had picked up, absent-mindedly, on his way out of the store. "A Beginner's Guide to DIY, easy steps for first time builders".

Hmm... I don't think I ever had the instruction manual for that pool table. There's bound to be something in here that'll gave me some pointers on how to dismantle it. Who knows? I may even be able to turn it into something else... maybe a nice bed, so I can stop sleeping on the floor for once.

After a quick read, Finn put the rest of his shopping away and decided to start planning, writing a list down of what he needed with a pen and a scrap of paper. Halfway through, he stopped and reread his shopping list, thinking it over.

All of this stuff... and even after I buy all of it, will I really have the patience to put it all together? No, I'm not going to be able to manage this at all. I might as well save myself the hassle and just make do with what I've got.

After scrapping his plans and turning to unpack more of his shopping, he cursed upon discovering that he hadn't picked up another carton of milk to replace the one which had expired the day before, and was about to head back out to get it when he was disturbed by a slow and deliberate sound, which came slithering into his home uninvited...

Creeeeeeeeaaaaak

The noise had come from his front door. More specifically, it had come from his letter plate, which had been in dire need of oiling since the day Finn had moved in but was never a top-priority on Finn's list of concerns. Putting down the pen and paper slowly, Finn stealthily moved to the wall which separated his living space from the entrance and peeked around the corner. The flap on the letter plate was being held open by someone on the other side.

Who in the eff is that!? What does he think he's doing, playing with my door!?

Finn was furious now. He was just about to march over and give this intruder a piece of his mind when the stranger's voice, or rather voices, emanated from the letter plate.

'Fiiiinn… We know you're in there. We've got a surprise for you!' came a sing-song voice from the door, to a chorus of sniggering.

Finn froze in place and waited, then there was a muffled slap from behind the door.

'You're not supposed to say his name, you nonce! Now he'll get suspicious!'

Finn was already suspicious, but now he was also panicked.

So, it's not just one guy? And they know my name? They must be the landlord's boys. Well, this is what I get for not paying the bloody rent. Okay, do I have any money on me? If I give them what I've got now, maybe they'll go away.

Upon leaving his hiding spot by the wall and making his way over to the counter where he had placed his wallet, Finn failed to notice that he had just stepped into the direct view of whoever it was that was currently looking through the letter plate.

'There he is! Oh boy, I'm getting pumped already! C'mon boys, lets break down this door and grab 'im!'

The level of excitement in this voice was only matched by the aggression of the one which came after it, from an older and harsher-sounding stranger than the first one.

'Well, we're going to have to, now that you can't keep your damn trap shut! I suggest you get out of my bloody way, before I break you down with it!'

Finn's mind went into overdrive and he tensed up with the phone in his hand.

Okay Finn, they're going to try and bust their way in now, so do I wait and give them the money, try to fight them off, or run away like a coward? Which is it gonna be?

The door shook and the letter flap clattered as something heavy collided with it. There was no telling whether the door would be able to last a few more hits like that.

Bloody hell! As if that's even a question I'd ask myself right now! Time to get out of here!

From his state of panic, Finn slipped on the cluttered floor. Then he grabbed his wallet and turned to the back window. He was on the first floor, but there were bushes right below his apartment. Of course, they were full of brambles and Finn didn't like the idea of having to land in them. But at least it would still be marginally better than flat concrete.

Another loud bang came from the front door, along with the sound of the wood splintering and the hinges crunching. Finn checked out of the window to see if there were any more dangers outside. Nothing. But with the sun now low it was hard to tell if there wasn't somebody hiding behind something. A third blow buckled the door. Cheering followed. He gave all it took to push aside that fear and focus on getting away from the more immediate threats. Working as fast as he could, Finn slid the window open enough to slip through, and began to crawl through it. He had just about made it through when something hard and fast burst through the glass above him with a tumultuous crash. This caused him to lose his balance, tumbling head first out of his window along with a shower of deadly shards.

Cut and bruised from the fall, Finn's list of concerns and his inner debate over which had been worse, the fall or the landing, were having to take a backseat to a more primal need that he never thought would end up needing. A need to survive. Pushing through the pain, Finn picked himself out of the thorn bush, wincing as he removed a stray, prickly stem which had wrapped around his arm during his landing. It left him flecked with small pricks and scratches. But the more pressing injuries had come from the glass, which had left a few larger cuts. Nothing that he would bleed out from and nothing embedded, but the pain and the blood enveloped him.

Yeah… getting out of there using the window, that was a good idea. If I'd stuck around, they would have killed me! I know that being behind on my rent was a bad move, but where did Steve find these animals?!

After he was free from the brambles and out onto the pavement, Finn looked back up to where his apartment was, just in time to dodge another of what had been thrown at him the first time. There was an intruder in his home, looking down on him from the shattered back window with a pool ball in his hand, which he had taken from the table in the entrance. The intruder's face was covered by a strip of cloth and a hood.

'Hey down there, coward! Come back up here, let's have a game!'

Finn was far too shocked to even attempt to try to communicate with the one who had broken into his home and ran around the corner to get to where his car was. When he rounded the corner, Finn heard an uproar from the balcony of his apartment complex. As he kept running, it was evident that the other pursuers were already aware of his escape and were scrambling to get to the ground floor and catch him, for whatever cruel intentions they had in mind.

That's when it appeared.

He heard at first the roar of its engine, and soon after, out of the corner of his eye he saw it. A huge, familiar white van had just pulled up behind him, after bouncing over the curb and onto the footpath, and it was gaining on him. Visions of last Friday and the kidnapping flashed before Finn's eyes, and he broke into a sprint, trying to get to his car as fast as possible. Upon doing so, Finn desperately fumbled with his keys and threw himself inside, just as the van rammed his rear bumper, destroying the left-side's tail lights and rocking the car horribly.

Finn cursed loudly, and fueled by adrenaline, twisted the keys in the ignition and slammed his foot down on the accelerator, as another ball from his pool set collided with his back windscreen. This caused a massive spider's web of cracks to form on the surface of the glass. Behind him, the van was reversing for another assault and the home invaders on foot had just got down the last set of stairs and were running right for him. Finally, Finn praised his car as his efforts to get it started kicked in and let him shoot out of the driveway with the van trailing after him.

'Oi! Are you just gonna bloody leave us here then!?' One of them shouted after the van in a fit of panic.

Finn's car and the van pursuing it left behind nothing but their exhaust fumes, picking up speed as they left the apartment complex and raced out of sight. The ones who were left standing on the driveway – the three masked assailants who had conspired to break into Finn's home – huddled together.

'And there he goes again, thinking he's Captain Amazing and racing off to save the day, when it was really us three who did all the real work.'

The tallest of the three glared at the speaker from under his hood.

'Oh really? Well, it looked to me like the only real work you were doing was to turn this whole thing into one giant dog's dinner! What did you think throwing those balls at him and running your mouth was going to accomplish, eh?'

The first speaker placed his thumb and forefinger on his chin mockingly and the third of the group, who hadn't spoken yet, desperately started signing for him to stop.

'Well, you see, it was all for dramatic effect! Gotta put fear into the guy so he makes plenty of mistakes.'

The taller intruder paused for a moment in the middle of his rage and calmly placed a hand on his partner's shoulder.

'Well, I suppose if it was for dramatic effect then I'll apologize—'

A sucker punch from the taller stranger connected with the shorter one, making him fall down clutching his face

'When hell freezes over! Learn to stop doing things just for the hell of it!'

'Bwaah!?!'

The third intruder drooped slightly in disappointment and walked over to help him up.

'See what happens? I tried to warn you it was a bad idea...'

'Ugh... Ow. Just help me up, okay?' The speaker mumbled, removing his mask and using it to hold his bleeding nose.

Both of the smaller figures looked to the other guiltily and waited for him to speak.

'So, here's what I want you to do: You there can go inside and try to find out whatever you can about places he might be headed to if our driver and his pal don't end up catching him before they get back. And you, Mr "Dramatic Effect", you can go and find those lost balls you threw around' The tall intruder commanded, pointing at each of the others in turn.

The intruder with the nosebleed coughed a few times before he responded with watery eyes.

'What for?'

'Pool. What else? Or maybe you would prefer me to keep pummeling your face for entertainment until they get back.'

'Alright, alright! Point taken!'

The sun had sunk below the tree line at this point, and the shadows of dusk began to envelop the countryside. Just down the road from his home, a bloodied and bruised Finn was flooring it to get away from the van which was chasing him. Judging by what had happened earlier, if it had a chance to catch up then there was no doubt that it would try to run him off the road. Looking in his left wing mirror, he saw that there was a driver, looking on at him with a kind of mad determination, and a passenger who was fumbling around with something behind his seat. Up ahead was the entrance onto the motorway. There he was sure that the top speed of his car would easily be able to outrun the van... But something was wrong. The passenger was doing something, something that Finn knew he wasn't going to like. It was a fear that answered itself when he tried to see what they were doing in his left wing mirror only to see it being blown clean off. It sounded like a clap of thunder.

Are you kidding me! That was a gun! Why do they have an effing gun?

The driver of the van swerved slightly, gritted his teeth and yelled at the passenger, who was leaning out of the left-side window and levelling a hunting rifle at the car in front of him, he was wearing a pair of ear muffs along with the same face mask as the others.

'Warn me the next time you do that will you? You're going to make me go deaf!'

Distracted, the rifle wielder pulled back one of his ear muffs.

'What was that you just said?'

'I said that—'

'Shut your face.'

'With a loud pop, another shot ricocheted off the back of Finn's car causing some dismay to the driver of the van, but mostly to the dismay of Finn, who was not at all comfortable with the added pressure of being shot at while trying to get away from someone. The turning for the motorway was about to come up, just a bit further and he could get out to the open road, where he could speed away from them and get out of range. That was where Finn found a problem. If it was just the van to worry about then the motorway would be perfect, but at this time of day it was too open. It would only be a matter of one well-placed bullet to stop his car, and being out in the open made that all the easier. Finn concentrated and pushed on forwards, going past the slip-road and flying towards the next town over, a rural village that he knew had a lot of stone structures, fences and buildings. That would do the trick. In the meantime, while Finn and the van chasing him raced on an overpass, the rifleman fired another three shots, two hitting the car, putting a dent in the right-side pillar and another breaking through the already cracked back windscreen and embedding itself in the back of the passenger-side headrest, causing Finn a great deal of anxiety. The close call had prompted the driver of the van to begin another round of arguing with his passenger.

'Hey! Mud-for-brains! Take off your damn earmuffs and listen to me!'

Annoyed by being distracted a second time, the rifleman wound himself in from the window and pulled off his headwear completely.

'What is it now!?'

'You will listen and you listen good! We're not trying to kill him, go for the bloody tyres and shoot straight this time!'

'Yeah sure, I'll shoot straight just so long as you can drive straight,' the rifleman exclaimed sarcastically, putting his earmuffs back on, and leaned back out of the window again.

'Bellend.'

'I heard that!'

Another shot scraped against the metal on the side of Finn's car, putting another gash in the paintwork as he swerved left to take a turning onto a side-road. The pursuers followed suit, and both of them kept up their acceleration. That last shot hit lower, they were getting smart, and that was bad news for Finn. This next road which they had turned onto was typical of its sort, winding and narrow, with trees on one side and a fence made from plates of stacked stone on the other, separating the road from a farmer's field. There wouldn't be enough room for another car to pass them if one happened to come the other way, heightening the danger. This was a fear which was going to become a reality sooner, rather than later. By looking across the fence and over the farming grounds, he could see where the road curved to the right by following the line of the stone fence, and up ahead there were headlights traveling in the direction towards where Finn was going. That said "collision imminent".

Okay! Don't panic, this is all going to be about timing. I know this road, there's a passing just a little further ahead, and if I get there at the right time, then I can pull in and dodge it. If not then I'm just going to have to hope that I can scrape by.

And now the part that Finn was dreading. In order to squeeze by the vehicle, which was steadily getting closer at the passing that he was thinking of, he was going to have to speed up, so he stepped up the acceleration, tearing around the curve dangerously while he gripped the steering wheel hard. When the headlights of Finn's battered, orange automobile intersected with those of the looming shape that was bearing down on him, he had only moments to react, and used them to quickly duck into the passing, just as another shot was fired from his pursuers.

Finn didn't see what happened to his pursuers, but he heard the screech of tyres and the sound of something crashing behind him. Nevertheless, he drove on, flying around the corner, out of the single-lane road and into the village, where he zipped and dodged around the foliage and rural architecture until, in a moment of blind faith, he checked his top mirror, fearing the worst but hoping for the best. That hope poured over him like a ray of sunshine after a long, stormy night. The ones who were chasing him were gone, nobody was shooting at him anymore, and for the first time all evening he could take a breather. Pulling in next to a small cottage, Finn parked and laid back in his seat, taking deep, wheezing breaths while he closed his eyes shut and tried to stop his hands from shaking.

Holy cow, that was intense... How the hell did this happen to me? They wanted to kill me. They had a gun and everything. Is a bit of unpaid rent all it takes to make somebody want to flat-out try to murder me?

Burying his face in his hands, Finn tried to wash the troubling thoughts from his mind, and in doing so was only reminded how badly hurt he still was. He looked over his arms and found that they were soaked with his own blood, matting the hair on his arms together. His head and around his neck also had oozing scratches, and when he cupped his face with his hands, some of the blood had been transferred onto it. His face felt wet and sticky. The cuts stung and his whole body felt sore, not only that, but he was starting to feel weak.

'All this over money, I mean, seriously...? I've gotta get myself some help,' Finn muttered under his breath.

After opening his car door, Finn nearly fell out, having lost blood and exhausted his boost of adrenaline meant that the lethargy hit him like a brick, and he stumbled while trying to walk straight. Resolving that nobody would try to steal his car knowing the state that it was in, Finn left the driver's door wide open while he dragged himself around the side of the cottage towards the front door, briefly tripping over a potted plant, before picking himself back up and feeling around aimlessly for the knocker, until after a few seconds of fumbling, realised that it did in fact have an electronic doorbell. Ushering up the strength to stand, he held himself and waited for an answer.

When the door was answered by its resident, he was already feeling much weaker. Finn couldn't make them out clearly, but could see that they were skeptical of him, opening the door just a crack to ask him who he was and why he was here. Unfortunately, the moment that he noticed the blood, the door slammed shut, followed by the sound it being bolted from the other side. Finding that getting the attention of this resident was as far as his strength would take him, and after turning away from the door in an attempt to leave his front garden, Finn found that his legs would not take him far before he collapsed and slumped down next to the wooden gate, listening to the sounds of crickets chirping and the below of distant car engines, while the cool evening air brushed over him and his breathing slowed, before he eventually slipped into unconsciousness.

'I've got you now, you slippery weasel!'

A hand reached out sharply from under the shade of the midnight woods, and grasped at the back collar of a man who was wearing a set of working overalls and a flat topped hat, who yelped in shock as he was yanked backwards and kicked on the back of his legs, causing him to fall to his knees.

'Wha...!? What in God's name are you doing!? Who are you people!?' The farmer exclaimed in distress.

A second assailant appeared in front of him, stepping around his associate, and pointed the barrel of a rifle just above the man's cheek. He was wearing red plastic earmuffs, which seemed to distract from the rest of his apparel, which was all black, and would otherwise make him very hard to see at this time of night. Neither of their faces could be made out behind the bandanas and hoods, which they were both wearing.

'Oh, it's all just noise with you people all the time, just shut up and stop moving.'

The farmer hadn't made it far from the road in his attempt to escape the gunman and his partner, his truck was left abandoned with its driver's door open. A bullet had punctured a hole in the bonnet and the front bumper had crumpled after their van had collided with it. Soon after the collision, the farmer had noticed the duo's intent and had chosen to try to flee into the neighbouring woods.

'Now here's how it's going to work. My buddy here is going to tie your hands and we're gonna have a nice stroll on down to the next town along to have a looksee for our friend who you helped get away, and when we find him then we'll all have tea and biscuits and hug it out, and then we'll send you on your way. Sound good?'

The farmer looked at the speaker in terror. He could feel how close the barrel was by the warmth which radiated from it.

'Can't you just let me go home?'

'Hey! What did I just say about "no talking"?'

As the man cowered, his hands were zip-tied behind him and he was forced onto his feet before being escorted to the back of the damaged van and thrown in through the back doors. The farmer only managed to get one quick shout out before the doors were slammed shut and he was locked away.

'Well, if we don't manage to find Mr Lacksley tonight, at least we can say we bagged someone to drop off for them. Do you think that'll keep them happy until he crops up again?' the rifleman queried, as they made their way to the front of the van.

'You think just one guy will do it for them do you? We wrecked the van, lost our target, and unless we catch him, then the guys downstairs will have our heads on a silver platter!'

'Oh, cheer up, you git! We're playing hide-and-seek with the guy who drives around in that ghastly orange thing, he might as well have a great, flashing sign over his head saying "Here I am!"'

The driver glared at the rifleman as they entered into the driver and passenger seats, with the rifleman shoving his firearm back behind his seat, and then they both closed their doors.

'Yeah sure, "hide-and-seek", my favourite next to "wild-goose-chase" and "catch-that-hobo". This is not a fun evening.'

'We still do a far better job than the "trio of terror" we left back at the apartment,' the rifleman rebutted.

'That reminds me, if we don't catch our target then we're gonna have to go back for them and brave the embarrassment from them as well,' the driver replied despondently while turning the keys in the ignition, and started moving the van around the crashed truck.

'I don't see why we should, they mucked up catching him at his apartment, so if anything, I'd say that it's more their fault than ours.'

The driver revved the engine angrily as they left the farmer's truck behind and headed up the road towards the next village.

'You just don't get it do you, bellend. That spot you're sitting in right now used to be for another guy, the tall bloke in the back used to know him as well, and one day he decided that he had enough of this life of stealing people away, and went downstairs to ask the guys we work for to let him off. We never saw him again. These people don't care whose fault it is, they will make us disappear if we mess this up.'

The gunman slouched in his seat and rested his head on one hand.

'Sure, I believe you, but you've got to stop being such a pessimist. We'll find him'

'I should bloody hope so.'

CHAPTER SEVEN

Waking up, Finn noticed he had been sleeping under a ceiling of white plaster with a floral design. Looking down, he could see that the walls had a striped pattern of white and pale green, and there was a lot of antique furniture dotted about the room. On one table there was even an old gramophone and a collection of vintage vinyl records. When sitting up, Finn found that there were some blood marks on the bed, but his injuries had been quite well bandaged. His wounds were sore and he still felt very tired from last night, but he was glad that somebody had gone out of their way to help him, even if he didn't know who it was. After lying on the bed and contemplating what he would do next for a while, Finn heard the catch on the door which led into the room being opened, and an older man walked in, holding a large bottle of water in both hands. He looked wizened, but not so much as to suggest a lack of mobility, glaring at him as he entered.

'Woken up have we? So, what are you, a fugitive or something?' the man asked while passing the water over to Finn, who sighed and accepted it from him.

'I don't even know, man… I got into my apartment late last night, and these guys turned up outside and tried to bust their way in. When I got out, they started chasing me down the road. I barely got out alive. Might have been debt collectors from my landlord, but... how aggressive they were just doesn't make sense.'

The older man pulled back the curtain to one of the windows for a moment and looked outside.

'Humph. I take it that they were the same lot who busted up your car, the little orange one round the corner which had been shot to pieces?'

'That's right, I've got no idea if they're going to try and come back for me, or how long it will take before I can go back home. I just—'

'Drink,' the man interrupted, nudging the water bottle towards Finn, who took a couple gulps of it and paused to catch his breath.

'If you've lost blood then you need to get your fluids back,' the man insisted.

'It's no use just bandaging you up and not putting anything back in, and don't you mind the car, I put a tarp over it while you were out cold.'

Saying that his car was taken care of alleviated some of the worries for Finn, but the mystery of why it had happened in the first place still hung in the room like a bad smell. Finn had been taken in, cared for, and hidden from the people who were looking for him, and didn't even know the name of this gentleman. It was a forgotten formality which he was obliged to correct.

'Just Harry will do, this is my house, and I served five tours as a field-medic. That's about all you need to know about me.'

'I'm sorry about this Harry, this is a lot to just drop on someone at short notice.'

'You've got that right, in fact, I wasn't going to do any of it, but with you passed out on my grass outside, I couldn't just have the neighbors popping over and seeing you lying there, cut up like a murder victim. What do you think they would have thought of me?'

Finn considered this and came to a conclusion.

'You're right, I'm going to be a burden here and probably put you in danger as well, I need to sort myself out and leave.'

When trying to stand up, the old veteran gave Finn a harsh glare and motioned for him to lay back down.

'You're not going anywhere until you're properly healed. Just keep drinking and lie back until your injuries have closed all the way, and don't tell me that I don't know what I'm doing. Five tours,' the man asserted, exerting his authority.

Unwilling to risk an ear lashing from this stern elder, Finn shifted in the bed and returned to his resting position, then he took another swig of the water, which seemed to make Harry a little less agitated.

'I'll be back in a bit to bring you breakfast, and I shall know if you've moved,' he stated, and left the room, pulling the door closed.

Ex-military?

It's probably a good thing that I ended up here. If he had just called an ambulance, then what's to say that they wouldn't be able to find me at the hospital and kill me there?

Finn put the water down for a moment and, after a small amount of fidgeting, took his phone out of his pocket.

Maybe I'm being paranoid again, but I would like to have at least some clue as to why they would chase me all that way. If it was just money that they wanted, all they had to do was scare me off and ransack the place, but they were out for blood!

Checking through his phone for his recent activity, Finn was drawn back to the pictures which he had refused to get rid of, and was reminded of when he was confronted about them by that stranger from the office department. The worker's panic and desperation had become a haunting memory to him, and the suggestion that the two events were connected cast a cloud of doubt over Finn's mind.

Sure, that was weird, but it wasn't "chasing me down the street, trying to blow my head off" weird. Am I supposed to believe that boring old warehouse 12 has some big secret that they're willing to kill their own employees for? It wouldn't be them. Just suggesting that is ludicrous…

After Harry had returned and gave Finn his breakfast, they sat and talked for a while. Finn spent most of the day in bed, recovering and having his bandages changed, and in the meantime, told the old veteran about some of his interests, while the old-timer shared stories from his service. While Finn's topics weren't particularly interesting, the man still listened patiently, which portrayed to Finn that, while he wasn't particularly happy to be looking after someone who just turned up on his doorstep, he at least appreciated the company.

'Do you know anything about the people who went after you? '

Finn shook his head.

'Not much, I can only guess that they're after some money I owe… Debt collectors, crazy ones'
'Ah well… I'm going to make us dinner, I'll give you a shout when it's ready. As for this problem, I'm certain we will need to get the police involved'

Hearing the door close once more, Finn felt that he had been lying in bed for a while now, and that it would be a good time to test how much he had recovered. Getting up, he found that his injuries didn't ache as much as they did in the morning, and he had a lot more strength to move around than he did at the end of last night. Truthfully, his injuries hadn't been as severe as he had first thought, it had only been the continued stress and exhaustion that caused him to pass out the day before, and having spent the time to re-stock on liquids and get his energy back, he was already starting to feel a lot better. Moving around the room, he took notice of a few things that he could see about the place. Behind the curtain he could see where his car was, it had been moved to a shaded spot further along the road and had a large, green tarp completely covering it.

I've got to thank him for that when I get the chance, I wouldn't be able to tell that it was the same car at first glance… I can't leave in it just yet, I need to be sure that these guys who are after me are long gone, so that I don't get chased down again. After that, I should go back home and take a tally of the damages.

When Harry returned with the tea, he was surprised to see that Finn was up and about, but understood that if he had regained enough strength to move around, then he was probably a lot closer to being fully recovered than he had first thought. After tea and dinner, Harry insisted that Finn would stay during the night, and that he would telephone the police to see if they could help him with getting his home back and taking him out of danger. Just one more night, and it would be a matter of explaining what went on to the authorities and finally, Finn could get his life back on track…

Half past two in the morning. This wasn't supposed to be a time where anything went on, especially on a Sunday. Everyone was asleep, so why did it mean anything to Eric Jones? Truthfully, he didn't expect to get anything out of it, his place of work had a clear and understandable schedule with a start and a finish time, it didn't run through all hours of the day, which was precisely why that time had stuck out to him. If he wanted to come away from this practical joke that he had fallen into for good, then the only way to prove those malicious documents and the pranksters who made them wrong, was with proof.

Eric got up in the night, just after half past one, and put on his work clothes. A recurring pattern in the documents had been a time stamp, showing hours of arrival between two and three o'clock, and all during the weekend. This was odd, considering that the warehouse and others of its sort would surely be closed and locked up at that time. If he were to arrive and the place was still locked shut with nobody in sight, then he could go back home knowing that whatever they had planned in the long run, wouldn't be something that he would fall for. Still, Finn had been harsh, and even mocked him for thinking that something was actually going on. Eric only had to imagine the kind of shocked expression that he would get out of Finn if he got there and some kind of weird experiment was going on with that equipment that he saw in the pictures, after working at Warehouse 12 for however many years and not knowing about it. That would surely give him something to be scared about. The thought spurred Eric on as he crept down the stairs with his backpack slung over his shoulders. The rest of his family would be dozing off at this time of night, so he made sure to stay silent while he made his way down and into the kitchen, where he opened the fridge and took a couple of snacks and a drink.

Eric's plan was to be there until three, as that was the latest that the logs showed on the papers, and he didn't want to go without packing some "provisions" in case nobody showed up.

Well, let's be honest here, if somebody does open the place up and drop off, say, a load of giant syringes and buzz saws welded onto robot arms, or one of those dentist chairs that they use to strap a person down so that they can't escape, I'd probably piss myself, but the likelihood of that happening? Slim to none, Eric mused.

Zipping up his backpack and putting on his favorite hat, a snug-fitting, brown beanie, he headed to the front door with a stealthy approach, being extra careful to open and close it slowly and silently. He slipped out of the house and into the cool, shadowy night without hearing a peep from the rest of his family, walking away from his home and towards the bus stop with purpose. It appeared that Eric had picked the right time to leave, as a bus was just pulling up as he got to the stop. Unsurprisingly, there wasn't anyone else besides himself and the driver on the bus. It was quiet besides the low rumble of the engine and the whoosh of trees and buildings passing by, and after ten, maybe fifteen minutes of sitting and waiting to arrive, he was there, just outside of work and he could see that the grounds were just as empty and lifeless as he had expected them to be at this time of night. After stepping off of the bus and watching it drive away, Eric's attention turned back to the warehouse, and he sighed, considering whether this was truly the best way to uncover what was really going on.

Just an hour or two I'll be here, and if no one shows up, then I can just head back, and nobody has to know that I was gone. I've brought a comic and some snacks with me so that I don't get bored, and... The gate is open?

The gate was open. The chain and padlock were on the ground nearby, and the front gate was pulled back, but after a quick inspection, Eric found that there was nobody parked inside.

Weird. The last few days, I always saw a guy come down and lock that gate while I was waiting to catch the bus home. At the time that he does it, nobody else is supposed to be left inside. Who would come along to unlock it in the dead of night if nobody is here to work?

There were no lights on, in or outside the building, the truck bays were empty, and the only sounds that could be heard were from distant cars further up the road and birds in the woods nearby. Eric felt ill at ease as he reluctantly entered through the front gate, feeling like he was a trespasser in a place where he didn't belong.

This is just going to be a little test; I'm not going to stick around any longer than I need to. I'll find who opened the gate, ask him about what happens at this time of night, and then I'll be on my way. I'm not trespassing, I'm in my work uniform, they'll understand.

Getting to the staff entrance, Eric looked around to see if there was anybody nearby yet, and when he was satisfied that the bay was vacant of anybody else, he swiped his entry pass over the electronic card reader and entered into the building. The locker room and connecting hallway were completely devoid of life. It was eerily quiet and had an unsettling atmosphere which permeated the interior of the building, it would have already been cool, on a day as overcast as today, as there was no central heating throughout the whole warehouse, but at night the temperature dropped a few degrees more. There wasn't much light inside either, the only illumination that could be felt from the first hallway that he travelled down was from the street lamps outside, which filtered in through dust-clogged windows and settled on the far wall. When Eric got to the end of it, he could no longer make anything out clearly, and so he opted to use the flashlight on his mobile phone to see into the choking shadows of the main section of the building – the factory floor. It was a large, empty space with a roof that went far up, to the point where the little light from Eric's phone wasn't enough to reveal what was up there. The usual shapes of working equipment, shelves and goods, some packed and some not, cast sinister shadows away from Eric and moved with him, drawing closer and retreating as he turned the light this way and that. Usually, this place would be filled with noise and activity, it would have the atmosphere of a place that, while monotonous and somewhat crowded was full of life, but in this state it was dead.

Jeez, this is not a good place to be. I have to feel sorry for whoever has to come in and work at this time of night when it's so dark and quiet, you could seriously hear a pin drop in this place...

After a begrudging search around the area that he would have been working during the day and making a quick stop at the water cooler to pick up some plastic cups, Eric decided to work up the courage to check some of the places that he hadn't been to yet, and almost panicked when an idea hit him.

Cameras. I can't believe that I didn't even think about it! If I was caught on camera, then I'm going to be in so much trouble! But... Maybe they're not on? I need to find out where they are so that I can be sure...

Going down another ghostly corridor, Eric pressed on to find out where the room with the camera screens would be, passing various departments on the way.

Processing, nope. Internal affairs, not that either. Basement? Not in a million years. Ah! Here it is, surveillance.

Feeling slightly guilty about being in a part of the building that he normally would never go, Eric pulled the door open just a crack, and was surprised to find that the screens for the camera system were still on and showing various locations around the complex, he then chose to enter the small room fully, switched the lights on inside, and pulled the door closed behind him. Most of the screens were painted over by the complete darkness which was ever-present in the building during the night, but a few still had enough light to show details. Strangely enough, the computer panel connected to them showed that none of them were recording.

They're on, but not recording. Phew, that is one worry out of the way at least. But why? Shouldn't they be recording all the time?

Eric was nearly at his limit when it came to discomforting discoveries at this ghost town of a warehouse. He shouldn't have been able to get in, let alone be able to wander inside and go places where he wasn't supposed to be, and things were out of place. It was like the building had been prepared for something to happen and then just left abandoned. There was no sight of any human beings on any of the surveillance cameras, not one soul.

Maybe... Just maybe, they didn't lock up properly the day before? Okay, I think I've had enough of this, this place is going to give me a heart attack if I stay here. I'll just say that this office prank is debunked and leave...

As Eric flicked the lights in the surveillance closet off and turned to go out of the door to leave, he took one last glance back at the camera screens, just as a last-minute precaution, and a detail which wasn't there before caught his eye. It was a set of headlights from a vehicle just outside of the warehouse, and it was steadily growing in luminosity, until it appeared from behind the wall which surrounded the outside of the complex. The headlights were bright and made it difficult to see the shape of what it was, but it turned into the truck bay and passed the camera's blind spot. Eric turned back and continued following the vehicle on another screen, this time showing a full view of the vehicle from the side. When it had parked, the driver and a passenger exited from their seats and made their way around to the back, where they opened a set of doors at the rear of the vehicle, and another figure stepped out with a flashlight. The last thing to leave the vehicle sent a cold shock down Eric's spine, and his eyes widened as he backed away from the screen in a moment of pure horror. A body, carried between two more passengers, was being lifted out of the back by their arms and legs, past the others, towards the one who had been driving, who had just scanned an entry card at the staff entrance. They then entered into the building as he held the door open for them.

What the hell! I knew something was going to go wrong, but not like this! I have to get out of here somehow...

Eric scanned the screens, looking for another way out of the building, a fire escape, anything that would get him out without being noticed, and after failing to find one, his panic turned to desperation.

There's nowhere to go, I'm blocked in from this side, and there's no way of me getting out from the front entrance. There's only one thing I can do, I don't want to do it, but what choice do I have?

Taking his phone out, Eric started to dial the one number that he knew would give him what he needed to find an exit. This was exactly the time that he would have called the police, seeing as whatever was going on was clearly a matter of some kind of criminal endeavor, but in the urgency of the situation, and with five of them out there who could find him at any time, the police would take too long to arrive. Instead, Eric dialed the number for his workplace mentor, which he had used to copy over the pictures of the documents which had started all of this, and waited in fearful anticipation while the dial tone sounded. The first time that he tried to call, the mobile phone rang out, and he was forced to try again, swearing under his breath as he redialed and prayed for Finn to pick up. After a few more seconds of waiting, that prayer was answered.

'I don't know who you think you are, calling me at this early in the morning but I have had a seriously messed up weekend, what do you bloody want?'

The chance that Finn knew another way out was enough to give Eric some hope that he could escape without being seen, and it was everything that he needed right now.

'Finn, it's me, Eric. I'm calling from work.'

'Eric? Oh lord, why do you still have this number? Don't you realize, the time is bloody gone past—'

'Finn, I messed up really bad! I'm trapped in here, and there are a bunch of guys who just went in as well, and they've got a—'

'Hey, slow down, don't start getting melodramatic. From the top, tell me what's going on.'

Eric's breathing was ragged from stress, but he had to explain his situation to his work mentor even if he was going to get rude, it was the only way.

'I'm at work. Nobody else was here when I arrived, but the gate was unlocked, so I just went in to see if the time on those papers was right'

'It shouldn't have been unlocked; you shouldn't be there. What about these people who arrived after you? What do they look like?'

'They uh...'

Eric tried to get a better look at the people who had now entered deeper into the building, and squinted to try and make out their faces.

'I can't tell who they are. They're not in uniform, just all black clothes, I can't see their faces.'

There was a short pause and then Finn resumed with his next question.

'Is there a van outside? Please tell me there isn't...'

Eric took another look at the cameras.

'Um... Yes, that's right... It looks a bit like it hit something as well at some point, 'cos the front looks a bit smashed in,' Eric informed him, hoping that it didn't mean that something terrible was about to happen and held his breath.

Finn froze. They had gone to where he worked looking for him, and by some terrible coincidence, that clueless, gullible trainee had turned up and got himself trapped inside with them. This was his fault. Instead of telling him to let go of the whole debacle over finding those reference papers and getting upset about them, he had just told him to do what he liked, and now it was going to come back and bite him for it. Finn didn't know what to say, he held the phone like it was glued to the side of his head and didn't say a word.

'Finn? I could really use some advice right about now,' Eric whispered anxiously over the phone.

'This is really stressing me out... This wasn't supposed to happen at all... Eric, listen carefully, where are you?'

'I'm in the surveillance room, the one with all the camera screens in it.'

'Can you see where they are?'

'Yes. They're halfway through the main floor, where all the stuff gets packed. I wanted to tell you before, but... They're carrying a body with them, but I don't know who it is, they might be dead!' Eric blurted out, losing his composure.

'Calm down! Listen to me, you're going to get out of here, alright? Just follow what I have to say.'

'Okay... But please, I don't know how long I can keep myself hidden here.'

'How is the corridor outside looking? Still clear?'

'Still clear,' Eric replied.

'Go to the end of the hall, opposite the way you came in, and take a left. There should be a fire exit that leads out to the back of the building.'

'Alright, I'm going.'

A fire exit was close by, that was a relief. Eric opened the door to the surveillance room carefully and peeked around the corner, nobody was there yet, but he could hear voices coming from deeper within the building. He decided that he would have to take the chance and get to the fire escape before they arrived. Jogging while trying to make as little noise as possible, he rounded the corner to the left. The fire exit was right where Finn had said that it would be, and he rushed over to it, brimming with excitement. Excitement which was swept away in a tide of dread, as the push-bar got stuck and the door refused to budge.

What the hell? It's not... it's not opening! It didn't even click. This door is locked!

Desperately, Eric fished back into his pocket and held his phone back up to his ear, and spoke to Finn, who was still on the line.

'Finn, this is a nightmare. The fire door won't open. Somebody locked it!'

'Locked? Bloody hell... Alright, this is going to be risky but I trust that you can get through this. Behind you there should be a set of double-doors which lead into the factory floor, if you entered in through the south side, then those doors should put you on the north side of the floor. Make your way back to where you came in from, and don't let them see you.'

Eric swallowed and took a look through one of the hard-plastic windows on the doors which led into the factory floor. There were two of them still inside who must have split off from the group, and with the voices he had heard earlier approaching close to the surveillance room where he had just been, there was no other choice, he would have to sneak past them. Opening one of the double-doors gingerly, he slipped in and stuck close to the shelving and obstacles which would shield him from sight as he made his way closer to the locker room. The strangers hadn't turned the factory's lights on, but they had torches of their own, and Eric had to duck behind a forklift while one of them flashed a beam of light around the room, he then pricked his ears and tried to listen in on what they were saying.

'What are you waving your light about for? Did you see something back there?' one of them asked the other, seeming to be genuinely concerned.

'I thought I heard something, could have been one of the other guys trying to sneak up on me. They know I don't like it when they creep around, but they do it anyway, just because.'

'Well, I don't really know what to tell you that'll help with that. They're not going to change, so I just try to do what I'm told'

'Yeah, that's all you ever do, isn't it?' The stranger spat, as his friend sagged his arms dejectedly.

Seeing that they were chatting amongst themselves and not focused on what was going on in the north side of the floor, Eric took the opportunity to move up.

'Okay, sorry. How's your nose doing?'

'How's my nose doing? How do you think it's bloody doing? It's smashed in, you nit!' the man barked.

'Sheesh! I was only asking because I was worried, is all...'

'Yeah? Well, isn't that nice. Seriously, this job could not be going any worse. For months, everything is fine and dandy, then all of a sudden it all goes tits-up!' the stranger complained, throwing his arms around.

'But we'll still find them, both of these fuckers, and when we do, the guys downstairs will be fine with us and everything will go back to normal.'

Guys downstairs? what could that mean? Eric pondered as he moved closer to his way out. By this point, he was nearly there.

'Well, you had better hope that we find them soon, because you don't want to know what they do to people when a job goes wrong and the target gets away.'

This seemed to have startled the other stranger.

'You know? Wha-what is it that they do?'

The intruder with the broken nose chuffed.

'Well, it only happened once, but when it did, they took the guy all the way downstairs, past the point where we get told to drop off targets, and do you know what they did next?'

'They... didn't kill him... did they?'

'No... Way worse... They shaved off his eyebrows! And he was so embarrassed that he ran away, and nobody ever saw him again!'

The other intruder dropped his guard, looking at the story-teller with an unamused expression.

'You're full of garbage...' He groaned, pinching the bridge of his nose.

It was during that awful joke, that Eric was able to pass from the factory floor and into the hallway leading up to the locker room, which he skimmed through silently, before he finally got to it, the last room before he could leave via the way he came in. He was home free.

Eric bolted out of the staff entrance, not caring if they heard him at this point, by the time they found out, he would be long gone. Thoughts raced through Eric's head as he ran past the van and towards the front gate; What would he tell his parents? Would he have to get a new job? Would he have to file a police report on what he saw? Would they believe him?

Of course, he would have Finn to back him up. It seemed to Eric that since he knew about the van, he had been in an encounter with them before, so that was someone who could vouch for him. However, it was just as Eric had reached the gate that he felt something was missing; his back felt light and unburdened. Trying to feel behind himself revealed to him that his suspicions were correct. He had taken off his rucksack and left it in the surveillance room.

I forgot my backpack? I can't think about that now, if they went inside and found it, then that means that I don't have any time to—

There was a crash behind him, it was the door to the staff entrance being thrown open. Losing his rucksack in the surveillance room might have just been the worst place, as all it would take was a quick look through the security screens to know where he was, and it had drawn them straight to him.

Lose...

All five of them were there, pushing to all try to get out of the door at once, but once they had, the chase was on. Eric ran like his life depended on it, because for all he knew, that was exactly the case.

CHAPTER EIGHT

C lattering and screaming. These were the last sounds that Finn heard coming from Eric's side of the phone call, and they had put him into a cold sweat. He had been so close to escaping from them, but somehow, the assailants who had once come after him had discovered Eric, and were now chasing him down. It sounded like he had dropped his phone, as the sounds of struggle were getting further away. How could he have let this happen? The guilt stuck in Finn like an icicle, and he sat up in bed, feeling nauseated by it. It was only by some miracle that Finn was able to get to his car in time, and Eric didn't drive. Even if he did, there was no doubt that that maniac with the rifle wouldn't let him get far, and with as much luck as himself. Finn stared into his hands, and with no response coming from the other side, and heavy regrets, he hung up the phone.

Damn! Damn it all! He wasn't even supposed to be there! Finn raged, throwing the phone down into his covers.

Eric was his trainee; he was meant to be responsible for him. Whatever he had been roped into, Eric was now a part of it, and all the blame was on Finn's shoulders for letting it get this bad, for being lazy and for being an awful mentor to him. It was from within Finn's lamentation that he decided he must do something about it personally, something that would put the pieces of this puzzle together. He would just have to hope that Harry would forgive him later for this.

That damned landlord had his goons chase me down, try to kill me, and now this confirms that they just kidnap people and do God knows what to them for fun?! This is insane!

Exiting the room where he had been spending his recovery for the last two nights, Finn checked around. There was a balcony which led down to the ground floor and a room closer to his, which he suspected to be Harry's bedroom. He checked that first. Thankfully, what he was looking for was right on the bedside counter, next to the snoring resident: Finn's car keys. They were resting in a small bowl on the counter alongside a desk-lamp and a few other trinkets, and would prove to be Finn's first hurdle when it came to fixing his ongoing dilemma, picking them up and exiting the house without waking him. Mercifully, and with a somewhat guilty conscience, this hurdle proved to be a small one. He retrieved his keys with ease, and left while Harry continued his deep slumber.

Poor guy... He stuck his neck out for me and I ended up having to cut and run on him... I've got to get moving now, if I don't get to Eric in time then they could kill him... They would kill him, anything to get to me... I know that this is going to get me in serious trouble, but I can't let myself be responsible for getting Eric murdered. I need to do this.

Letting himself out of the front door, Finn made his way down the road to where his car lay, battered by the last weekend's narrow escape and still covered by the tarp which Harry had provided. Finn hesitated a moment, considering the kind of danger he was about to embark on and what the future of his life could be should he fail, but pushed the thoughts aside, choosing instead to focus on the need to take back control as soon as possible, and that started with finding

Eric. He could only pray that he would be fast enough to outrun them, at least for long enough that he would be able to find him.

The tarp was pulled off, bundled away in the back seat and secured, before Finn got into his little orange automobile and started it up. The very early morning sky was a miasma of navy-blue stratus which hung over the countryside and seemingly threatened to crush the peaceful lands flat with an impending downpour at any moment. It would be the backdrop to Finn's perilous journey as his car's headlights could be seen leaving the vicinity of the old village where he had spent his last few nights, now he sped back towards his place of work, back to the place where he would meet with his fate.

The car rumbled as it travelled back down the winding roads of the rural area. Despite the damage, there was nothing particularly affecting the performance of the car, which was a blessing, because everything hinged on getting to the warehouse and getting out again as quickly as possible. Finn crossed back over the overpass and turned out onto the motorway.

He had arrived, and for what little of the warehouse was out of place, the differences were what made it all the more menacing. Eric was nowhere to be seen, but the van was there, the same one that had haunted Finn's nightmares since it had nearly been the end of his life on multiple occasions. He resisted the urge to get out of his car and slash its tires for good measure, but held his grief and waited. He couldn't hear any sounds of struggle, but could hear by the sounds of cheering and hollering that whatever the criminals had set out to do, at least something had gone right for them, and that was bad news for Finn, presumably worse news for Eric. After they would leave, Finn would simply have to investigate and find out what had become of him. While Finn was hidden with his car, parked inside the forest a long way back and covered back over with the tarp given to him by the old veteran, Finn spied on the van from his hiding spot, eventually giving up when his wait seemed to be going on for longer that he liked, and he decided to make his move, simply hoping that he wouldn't be seen.

Cautiously, he headed to the staff entrance and observed the door. It was standard for its sort; thick, wooden and secured with a key card lock, impenetrable without his entry card. Onto plan B. The canteen was, in essence disgusting, but it had been one of Finn's prime places to stash things that he didn't want to lose as a result of its off-putting reputation. Inside he found what he was looking for, a sturdy pair of heavy-duty working gloves and a set of padded overalls. It wasn't armor by any means, but if Finn was going to chance running into his "old friends" again, he wanted to be at least as prepared as he could get for what they would throw at him. The next part would be to get armed. Going back out, Finn rooted around in the discarded piles of metal outside until he found something that would suffice should any unlucky sod want to pick a fight with him.

Looks like this rebar here will do nicely. It's covered in rust, but feels solid. It's a good thing that I've got gloves for this. Tetanus for thee, but not for me, Finn mused while testing the weight of it.

Now would come the hard part: getting in. The staff entrance and back-door fire escape were alarmed, but it had struck Finn that he knew what wasn't – the steel curtains which covered the truck bays at night, and he knew just how to get one of them open. Further into the warehouse's entrance, there was a forklift, abandoned under an alcove, probably by a worker who was too lazy to park it inside. There was always one, and it would be Finn's ticket to getting in. Pulling himself up into the driver's seat, Finn felt a shiver of nervousness run through him. This would probably be the most criminal thing he had ever done, and his every action while operating it was mired in unease.

Oh, lordy me, this is actually happening. Finn, you absolute madman. Okay, all I have to do now is just line it up, nice and easy and... Oh God, I hate this part! AAAAAAAHH!!

Ramming it forwards as fast as the forklift would go, Finn managed to work up enough force to wedge the prongs under the steel curtain which lifted slightly with a horrible metal scraping sound.

Ooof... I didn't like that. It feels like my insides did a backflip... This is so stupid...

Finally, after collecting himself, Finn operated the forklift one last time and pulled the lever which would raise the prongs and the curtain with it. The wall of metal raised, groaning sharply and making Finn wince at the sound, before he decided that it would be enough to get in, and he left the forklift as it was.

And there we have it, plan B is a success. I am never doing that again.

Finn lay down on his front and shimmied his way under the steel curtain, trying desperately not to think of the prospect of it falling on him and cutting his body in half, until he was all the way through and took a wheezing breath of the old, dusty air, before the weight of the curtain eventually proved too much and the prongs of the forklift were pushed back down, swallowing back the last sliver of light which had filtered in from his point of entry. That was the point of no return. Anything that Finn did from now on was going to be solely for the purpose of his investigation, and it started with going over what he already knew. Finn hadn't heard everything that was said while Eric was escaping from here, but from what he had heard, there were things that stood out, the body for instance. Eric had claimed that he saw a body being unloaded from the van and that the thugs who had been bothering them both had their own key card. That was Finn's first clue, the people here didn't just hand out security passes to anyone, so they must have either stolen one or they were working with somebody on the inside, both seemed as likely as each other at this point, especially after Finn heard his second clue, a phrase that he had overheard from a couple of sentries who hadn't realized how loud they had been talking while Finn was still on the line with Eric.

"Guys downstairs" they said. That's ominous, really freaking ominous. It sounded like those are the people who Steve and his gang report to, however they ended up getting connected to whatever is going on here, and if I'm going with the presumption that they are working with somebody here, then there is only one place that "downstairs" could be. I just hope that however remote this chance it going to be, I'm in luck, and that's where he is... Or maybe all of the paranoia has got to me and I've developed schizophrenia. That sounds more likely.

Like Eric, Finn had never been inside the building past hours. He had no way of illuminating his surroundings besides the lighter which was on his person at all times. While making his way down the corridor towards the factory floor, Finn took out a cigarette and lit it, hoping that it would provide some relief from the stressful urgency to which recent events had unfolded.

Whatever happens here, whatever I see when I get down there, this is going to be the last time that I come here, to do my job or otherwise. And when this is done, I swear I am moving far away to somewhere on the other side of England, or further still... Maybe even jump ship from the UK entirely, and then it'll all be smooth sailing. Alright, let's get this done...

Finn's destination was the basement. It was the only "downstairs" in the whole building, and as it stood, the only place with which he had any hope of finding Eric, if indeed the masked strangers had taken him down there. Their reasons didn't concern Finn, he was coming to get Eric out of there and that was it, anything else was a problem left for another day. Passing through the cold and empty factory, Finn had to rely somewhat on memory to navigate it, as his source of light wasn't nearly enough to compensate for the all-consuming shadows which enwreathed every surface of the industrial complex, but his memory proved to be up to the task, and he found his way to the end of it. The next corridor was just as deserted as the first, and his footsteps echoed as he made his way down it and towards one of the doors on his right, marked as "basement".

The wooden door which proclaimed itself as the entrance to the basement swung open easily, which was something that Finn took as a sign that things weren't as bad as they seemed. If it had truly been the prelude to some horrible discovery, then it would have creaked like the opening of a coffin lid, or at least this was what the theatre of Finn's overactive imagination had suggested. Instead, it had opened without any real difficulty and barely a sound, and after finding the light switch, it revealed itself to be a plain, dusty storeroom, with a floor crisscrossed with yellow tape and arranged with shelving, packages in various sizes, and a small service elevator for moving goods to and from the lower floor.

Impossible... There's nothing here... No, there must be something here, I just need to take a closer look.

Travelling down the flight of steps which led into the lower level, Finn scanned around the room, looking for anything that might be out of place, a loose brick, a shelf that would pull back to reveal a secret passageway.

Anything.

He found nothing.

Breathing heavily, he leaned on the service elevator. It was small and looked to be designed to shift crates, rather than people and it was only after a few tries at the controls that he came to the conclusion that it was out of order, and made a horrible, gear-grinding sound when he pulled one of the leavers. Giving in to his frustration, Finn yanked hard on the leaver, pulling it down until something within the machine went clunk. There was another clunking sound soon after, louder this time, and coming from elsewhere in the room. Just as the first sound had died down, another took its place, a low rumbling which steadily grew in intensity.

Uh-oh. That sounded bad, but I didn't touch anything else, I just... Oh... You have got to be kidding me!

It was the floor. The very concrete floor which Finn was standing on began to depress and slide open at the seams where the yellow tape met and concealed its appearance. With a churning, mechanical sound, the hidden doorway came to a stop and presented the dark, secret depths which lay below to the unsuspecting ex-factory worker.

An actual secret lair... Unbelievable. Who the hell was hiding this right under my nose this whole time!? This just went straight from being a murder mystery, to comic book villains trying to take over the world just like that, zero to one-hundred!

Aside from joking with himself in order to cope with what he had just been presented with, Finn couldn't help but be plunged back into a familiar sense of dread. Whatever was below had no reason to be good, and as he mustered up the bravery to go on, Finn gripped the rebar in his glove tightly, and tentatively stepped down and into the unknown horrors which beckoned from deeper below. Before, Finn was in a place where he shouldn't have been, given both the time and the circumstance, but here, Finn was where he was sure no average worker in the factory above was ever supposed to be. This place was a dark secret, something that screamed to him the kind of danger that it entailed, but at the same time elicited a kind of dangerous thrill, what kind of secret was it that this place was hiding? What danger lurked in its depths? Finn was determined to find out.

After nearly a minute of traversing the steps which led down into this strange and foreboding part of the building, Finn came to a platform with two paths. On one side there were yet more steps leading further down, and on the other was a large and imposing elevator shaft, which by the size of it, looked to be built to transport many people at a time, as well as whatever heavy objects a person would need in the dubious enterprise which lay far below. Considering that he had a need to attract as little attention to himself from this moment forward as he could possibly afford, Finn opted to continue his journey into the earth the old-fashioned way and take the stairs. He might have been reckless in his entry into the building above, but when dealing with this new discovery, he would have to be on his guard at all times. Anything could be down there.

The stairwell was getting progressively colder the deeper Finn descended. It had already been somewhat cool in the building above but down here it was cold enough for him to wish that he had brought something much warmer to wear. The walls which Finn passed as he moved down, barely lit by the soft glow of his lighter's fragile flame, shifted from a more industrial dry wall, to a damp and stony texture, indicating to Finn that at some point, he would find himself within some kind of cave when he got to the bottom, and after traveling down for quite some time while he struggled to keep his footing on the moisture-covered steps, his suspicions turned out to be true.

'No Way... This is too much...' Finn breathed, as he took in the sight before him.

As the very last step which connected to this new area was dismounted, Finn stood and stared out into the sheer depth of the place. It wasn't simply a small cave like he had expected, it was a vast and sprawling cavern. The entirety of it must have at least covered the space of a small town and most of the floor was taken up by the presence of an expansive subterranean lake, which shimmered and sent waves of light up to the roof, making the stalactites which hung there, pulse and dance with the luminosity which it cast on them. Of course, there would be no light for the lake to reflect if didn't come from something man-made, this far into the depths of the earth. At the foot of the lake, a fair distance away from the place where Finn had entered, there was something like a collage of buildings, all built onto each other as if it had originally only been a small structure, but over time it had taken on numerous expansions with little regard for remaining organized, and so it had built additions anywhere that it had saw fit. The whole structure was lit from the inside and covered in a shell of scaffolding, by the looks of things it was quite active inside. Floodlights on the roof shone out onto the lake and used it to fill the whole cavern with light. A little way ahead there was a scene taking place, and Finn made sure to keep his distance as it unfolded, but pricked his ears to the distant voices which became more coherent as he approached.

Along the cave floor, there was a path which had been dug out of the rough stone and patched with planks of wood where gaps in the ground needed to be covered. Finn chose to stray somewhat from the path which had been built, as a means of getting to the building at the foot of the lake. At the current time, remaining undetected was still Finn's top priority, and he wanted to keep it that way in the absence of a better plan of action. Further along this path, there were seven people, many of them were hard to make out in the dim light of the cave but Finn could see that out of them, two were unconscious and being transported by the other five, until they had reached a platform halfway along the path. After traversing some of the uneven terrain of the cave floor, Finn settled down a short distance from the platform, where the lack of light and obscuring deposits of stone would mask his presence, and craned his ears to eavesdrop on their conversation.

'... So, we're done for the day now? We get to pack our bags and have the rest of the night shift off? I don't know about you, but that sounds fishy to me, we usually do the whole night—' one of the figures complained.

'Shut up,' another interrupted. 'If we're done for the day, then stop whining about it.'

'Hey! Was I talking to you? That's right, I wasn't, so just—'

'Do I seriously have to bash your heads together to get you two to stop acting like children?' rumbled a third.

The two who were arguing piped down and turned away from each other, and in the meantime, a fourth stepped up and spoke in a more cautious tone to the one who had broken them up.

'We, um... got one out of two for them... Do you thing that they'll be mad at us since we couldn't catch the other?'

The taller man glared at him and cracked his knuckles, causing him to cower slightly.

'You had better hope not. Anything that risks exposure is something that is more than likely to tick them off. So, when they arrive, we just hand them over and leave the talking to me.'

And so, they waited, the five of them stood around while Finn kept hidden from them, taking a peek every now and then to see if anything had changed. One of the figures had claimed that they had caught one out of the two people that they were looking for. That said to Finn that these were the same people who were looking for him, and that Eric, who they had already caught, was already one of their targets. Spotting him as one of the bodies that were lying down, this was confirmed to be the case, and thankfully at this distance, Finn could see his chest rise and fall.

What on earth have I got myself into? This is unreal. Eric is right there, but I can't just swoop in and get him out of here, I have to bide my time until there's an opening and then—

'Here they come! Lay out the targets and just do what they tell you to do, you morons!'

Finn's attention turned to further up the path, where four men, looking to be wearing some form of military attire, were fast approaching, carrying a pair of stretchers. With them was a fifth figure, who was seen to be an officer of sorts, and he did not look at all pleased as he stepped up to address the five kidnappers in black.

'These are the targets you were tasked with bringing to us? Identify them,' the official barked.

'One of two. This here is the Eric who you were looking for. Eric Jones, works upstairs. He was trying to sneak in after hours.'

'And the other?' he queried with more than a little menace in his tone.

'Nothing but a minor complication. Our van got damaged and he got away, but—'

The officer made a gesture to the other soldiers and then turned back angrily.

'But, nothing. You failed to catch a high priority target and you damaged a company asset! Am I to believe that after this time, you have forgotten the price of failure?'

The tall kidnapper fidgeted.

'No sir. We haven't forgotten.'

'Then hammer it in! Failure is unacceptable. In the event that someone leaks any form of sensitive data, you are to find those responsible and bring them to us. As you say, Eric Jones saw this data and had the curiosity to investigate. This is how a breach could lead to the exposure of our operation!'

'Look, we're sorry! There won't be any more failures, I'll make sure of it,' the kidnapper blurted out.

'You had better. Now I'm going to take these two inside and have a word with our superiors. Let it be known that there will be a form of punishment, but I will be lenient and do what I can to lessen the consequences of your mistake, which is a lot. In the meantime, find Finn Lacksley and do not fail again.'

'Yes sir. We will leave now. Come on! Let's not stick around and wait to see how pissed off they get! We're leaving!'

The tall kidnapper commanded the others, who were standing around, gawking or looking sorry for themselves.

As the five turned to leave, they left their captured with the soldiers and headed back towards the elevator, slinking away like shadows, and banished themselves amongst the indistinguishable darkness which lapped at the dome-shaped wall of the cavern. Whether the kidnappers would leave by the stairs or by using the elevator was no longer a concern of Finn's; what mattered now was, while one problem had been eliminated, another had just as quickly taken its place.

This is like a bad dream… I'm in this huge cave, miles under where I work… Those people that made my life a living hell are kidnapping people and bringing them here. Do they even still work for Steve? And now I have this to worry about, soldiers from some weird underground community… I need time to process all of this.

Even armed with the rusty rebar, Finn was sure that he wouldn't be able to take on five trained soldiers, even more than he would be able to deal with the five bloodthirsty kidnappers who had just left. What he needed was a distraction, something that would get their attention off of Eric for long enough that he could sneak in and get him out of there.

All I need is one moment, I don't care what they are doing, what their stupid operation is, I just want to get us both out of here alive and get back to my old life. Finn thought to himself as the soldiers and their officer carried the two unconscious prisoners back towards what Finn suspected was their headquarters.

Traversing slippery rocks and avoiding the many gaps along the floor of the cavern was a challenge, but it was one that Finn was prepared to take when it came to making sure that he avoided the lit path and kept up with the soldiers.

A challenge that he was not prepared to face however, was when upon entering into the hanger which presented itself as the entrance of the huge building at the foot of the lake, a pair of heavy bulkheads would close, allowing his last glimpse of Eric to be of his lying prone form being carried away on a stretcher, before Finn was cut off from the outside and left completely alone, and with nowhere to go.

CHAPTER NINE

The feeling that overcame Finn as he watched the bulkheads close in front of him was one of misery and of hopelessness. Standing in the dark of this beautiful cavern, which had been tainted by this Frankenstein's monster of a building looming over him, Finn lamented at the options which lay before him. Leaving now would be the safest choice, it would be the choice to cut his losses and ditch his associate in order to save his own hide. Just thinking about it made Finn feel wretched. As for his other choice, he would have to enter the building somehow and get out without alerting the whole place, a task which for him, would be tantamount to suicide.

He was no hero. How could he possibly accomplish something like this? Finn wracked his mind in an effort to come up with a solution to his plight, and was disappointed that the best he could come up with was to search the outer walls of the building for another way in and just hope that nobody would see him.

It would have been impossible for Finn to tell what the purpose of this facility was, or what the "operation" going on inside it could be; only that for a place this large, it must be something big, something that the people inside would consider to be extremely dangerous if it got out. Contemplating this only added to Finn's anticipation.

The outer walls were made of smooth sheets of plate-metal, dampened by condensation. Upon getting close to said wall, Finn hugged up to it and used the scaffolding to shield himself from view as he made his way around the left side, keeping his eyes peeled for signs of danger. After making his way around the building for a good minute or so, he came to a possible entry, although it was not one that Finn would have liked to consider. There were very few windows on the exterior of the building and the ones it did have were mostly on the upper floors, most likely as observation points for victims being dropped off. At this point of the complex however, there was a series of vents, feeding out of the side and working to filter the air within.

Air vents? This had better not be the best way in... I mean, I could get trapped in there and die. It wouldn't even be funny. Look, the fan blades are still going and everything!

No, today would not be the day that Finn would go traipsing through the ventilation ducts of this hazardous and unknown building. Even if he did, getting out with Eric in tow by using the same way in would be less than ideal, so he would keep looking. Further around the left side of the building was what looked to be a fire escape, but this came with its own problem, it was guarded. The one guarding the door looked to be on his break, wearing the same military-style clothing as the others Finn had seen, and was puffing on a cigarette.

Oh boy, well isn't that just dandy. My options now include either a choice of dangerous and stupid, or bullets. Thanks for the offer, but I think I'll take crawling through a couple of dusty air vents over being turned into Swiss cheese. Eric had better at least thank me for going through all of this for his sake.

And with that, it was back to plan A: the vents. Finn made his way back down to them and decided to make an examination of them before he would crawl in. The fan blades weren't spinning particularly fast, and he would be able to wrench one of them off with the rebar easily. He was far enough away from the guard that he wouldn't be in any danger of alerting him, so he took a few steps up to it and angled his makeshift weapon to strike at the fan blades. Before Finn swung down at the vent, he hesitated for a moment. Having noticed something out of the ordinary about it, he took off a glove and held his bare hand out.

It's cold... Actually no, scratch that, its freezing!

He put his glove back on and took another quick look around.

The interior of the cavern was already somewhat on the cold side, but the draft which blew out of these air vents was frigid, so much so that frost had formed on the metal. Finn couldn't fathom why a building so far underground would need to be kept even colder than the outside environment but nonetheless agreed with himself that he would have to push on regardless, and angled his stick of rusty rebar once more. Pistoning the length of metal into the air duct's rotating fan blade, Finn was successful at preventing it from spinning, and it came to a stop with a satisfying clunk. Next, was a matter of levering it off to give Finn enough space to climb in, this turned out not to be the greatest hardship for the master of destruction that Finn had become, and after taking one last glance to see that his entry had gone unnoticed, he slipped into the icy metal airways and made his way inside.

Scratching, clawing, scrabbling and screeching in their cages. All test subjects, past and future, living behind cruel steel bars, wire mesh and glass displays.

Prisoners, just like him.

He was in his 30s, of average height and dressed in a plain, grey shirt, jet black trousers and a long, white overcoat with flecks of dried blood on the ends of his sleeves. He sat in front of a long metal table filled to the brim with medical utensils, books and papers, cupping his chin with his hands and staring at the chart in front of him with a tired and melancholy expression. There were bags under his eyes, and his unkempt hair gave him a distinctly disheveled look; a sign that he had been working too hard, more than the result of the oppressing atmosphere attributed by the constant noise which filled his cell at all times. That was something that he was used to at this point. This man was somebody who didn't know where he was or how he got there, only that he had been exploited – his genius taken for granted as he slaved away for someone who had neither the patience or understanding to truly appreciate his work. And his work was his world, despite everything that had happened to him.

For now though, he had this to consider: a handful of his captors would be delivering some new subjects for the usual treatment, and the job would be passed on to his capable hands in order to carry it out, so he would have to get his equipment set up and ready for when they arrived. But it was hard to find the enthusiasm. Had he been doing this for so long that the marvels of his work were now nothing more than a chore? The man in the white overcoat stood up from his seat with a sigh of indignation and stared at the ceiling for a short while, before he began what would be just another of the same routine, where he would carefully arrange the equipment in his chamber for the application phase, perform what he considered to be the greatest feat of medical and scientific history since the discovery of penicillin, and then proceed to get absolutely no credit for his hard work whatsoever.

It was mind-numbingly depressing. It was almost like he was sleepwalking while he pieced together the seats and their restraints, folding down the robotic arm with the large hypodermic needle on the end and refilling the canister on the back with a fresh dose of something red and viscous which came from a carefully sealed case, exuding an icy mist as it was opened and closed. When he was done, he took a step back and looked over it all, then he imagined the person who had locked him away from the world, strapped in and unable to move a muscle as the needle came down and sealed his fate, while he could only cry out in fear over what would come next. The thought made him feel just a little bit warmer inside.

Behind the caged scientist, was a wall of steel bars and a door further along, at the back of the room, which led into his lab/prison. With little warning, a group of heavily outfitted men entered and gently placed down two stretchers holding a pair of sleeping figures. Behind them was a fifth who wore more officerial garb, who stepped up to the man behind the bars and read out from a sheet of paper in front of him in a monotonous, military tone.

'Good morning, doctor. On acceptance of these test subjects, you are authorized to perform one standard procedure, Class 1-A treatment on both subjects. Any divergence from standard procedure will result in termination of the test and immediate disciplinary action, that is all.'

Class 1-A – how they would ever expect him to learn anything new at all. The first few years had been taxing but insightful, when he was expected to routinely produce new results while cracking down on the flaws of the experiments which he had been assigned. As a result, he had taken his understanding of it all in leaps and bounds, but over the last few years it had all ground down to a halt. The people who had been holding him captive seemed to be more inclined to stubbornly believe that throwing the same scenarios at him, over and over, was going to result in something different and worthwhile to them. That or they were beginning to lose interest, which was worrying in of itself. Nevertheless, they had commanded that he start the procedure, and so he would, as if he had a choice in the matter.

The soldiers only helped to a point, getting the bodies of the unconscious soon-to-be test subjects carried into their seats and strapped in, before they took up positions along the walls to the right and left, watching him with anticipation. With a dreary voice, conveying some of his audible displeasure to the rest of the room, the man in the white overcoat announced the start of the procedure.

'...Alright, welcome to another Class 1-A treatment procedure. You all know how this goes. If you get squeamish at the sight of needles, then feel free to look away. Or, you know... Don't. It's not my problem to know what you want to do with your lives. The test is starting now,' he grumbled while spacing himself to make sure that all of them had heard him.

With his announcement over, the doctor walked over to a monitor which was set into the side of the chair to his right and flicked a handful of switches into their active position, then he listened as the contraption whirred to life, just barely audible over the din of his cell's less-human residents.

Eric's whole body felt sore, like he had just got mugged not too long ago. It felt like he was submerged in treacle, as he struggled to open his eyes and to remember what had happened to him. There also seemed to be something pinning down his arms or legs. He remembered running from something… He had gone to where he was working to find out about something which he had been involved in recently, when something went wrong and he had been forced to flee… He thought that he must have not been successful in getting away as he was now in his current situation, beaten up and unable to move. There was only one thing to do now, which was to open his eyes and try to find out where he was. Surely there was no harm that would come of that?

He couldn't have been more wrong.

When his vision came back into focus, it was like all of his nightmares had merged into one. The dentist chair, the needle, the evil scientist, and the sounds of distressed animals, hissing and shrieking behind him. Panic hit Eric like a tidal wave, and he tensed up at the horrors around him, feeling his heart begin to pound in his chest. The man who was about to perform whatever kind of morally ambiguous experiment on him turned to look him in the face for a moment and noted his renewed consciousness with an expression as if this was only a minor inconvenience.

'Oh joy, subject number two is awake… Please try not to scream while I am operating, it only agitates the pets more'

It seemed that saying this was rather pointless though, as Eric was going to scream anyway, making the animals behind him cry out even louder and rattle their cages. Eric's distress seemed to be affecting the others in the room as well, who shuffled uncomfortably.

'Doctor, may I remind you that you are obliged to accept assistance in anesthetizing patients, should it be required,' the one in the officer's uniform informed him, having to raise his voice to be heard over the volume of noise in the room.

'No, no... that shouldn't be necessary. I'll just have a talk with the fellow and we should be able to arrive at an understanding.'

Arriving back in front of the helpless boy, the doctor crouched slightly so that he was level with him, and started back up again, trying to sound as friendly as possible.

'Hello there, young sir! What's your name? You're just going to scream at me? That's fine, that's fine... I would like you to look at the chair to your left.'

Begrudgingly, Eric did as he was told, and saw an identical chair with a man strapped into it that looked to be wearing a farmer's overalls, a needle hovered menacingly above the underside of his left arm and there was a grid of laser lights shining onto it, which seemed to be a means of keeping the needle on target.

'I want you to see how quick and easy this procedure is, so that when it's your turn, you should have nothing to worry about,' the doctor said calmly, as he made his way over to the control panel on the side of the chair and pressed a button.

From the moment the doctor's finger depressed the key, the needle began to slide downwards, piercing the man's flesh and disappearing beneath his skin. When the needle was halfway embedded, it stopped and then the doctor turned a dial, making a strange, red liquid enter through the syringe and flow into the man's bloodstream. With the liquid emptied into the unconscious man, the procedure for his first subject was now complete, and the doctor removed the needle and turned off the machine, getting two of the soldiers in the room to bandage the still-unconscious man's arm with a small roll of cotton and medical wrap, before they took him away, leaving the doctor to make his way back to the terrified and quite conscious Eric, who stared at him with his mouth opening and closing.

The doctor looked down at Eric's arm, appearing to be making an observation.

'How interesting... A pre-existing injury. Loss of digits, four and five. Yes, I will have to log this down and monitor their development.'

'Please don't!' Eric pleaded, but this fell on deaf ears.

'You can close your eyes while it happens, imagine that you're in a nicer place, I find that tends to help—' the doctor reassured, before he was interrupted by the voice of the officer once again.

'Doctor, would you please get on with the procedure, we don't have all day to waste on coddling your test subjects.'

'Yes, yes... The procedure... Eyes closed, think of someplace else,' the doctor repeated before pressing in the button which caused the needle arm to descend on the hapless boy, who scrunched his eyes closed and prepared for the inevitable.

It's just like giving blood, just don't think about how much it's going to hurt... Oh God, why is this happening! Eric thought, as the needle pricked his arm and slowly worked its way in.

'There... the serum has been administered. We're just extracting the syringe now, and... Done. You can look around now.'

It was true that the whole thing hadn't been as painful as Eric imagined that it would be, but it was still the overarching horror of being injected with something that he couldn't fathom. He looked down to see the needle fully removed, his arm beading with blood, and his fingers twitching out of reflex, and fell into despair as his eyes started to water. Finally, looking back at the man who had performed this strange and deliberate act on him, with tears welling up in his eyes, he asked: 'Who… Who are you?'

To which the doctor replied politely: 'I am known here as Doctor Voe, but you can call me Andrew if you want.'

CHAPTER TEN

C ramped, cold and utterly fed up with this whole idea,
Finn Lacksley pressed on through the building's
ventilation system, hoping that at the end of his arduous trek,
he would come to meet up with Eric again, or at least find
something that would make travelling through the building
a bit safer, a disguise perhaps...

*Yeah, crawling in through the air vents. I'm sure that none of
them in here expected somebody to actually try applying cheesy
90's spy movie logic to real life as a way of breaking in,* he mused,
using his phone now to light the way, rather than his lighter.

*I'm just like a secret agent, except maybe just a bit colder
and smelling like a factory, but still... Agent Lacksley, Super
Spy.* He chuckled at his own joke, he had to find time for it
somewhere, as it took the edge off the insanity of what he
was doing.

While crawling through the vents, Finn took note that
every now and then, there would be a grate with slats which
he could see through. On the other side of most of these
grates was cold, concrete floor, white and undecorated walls,
and a serious lack of life. Finn had expected from what he saw
outside for it to be a building utterly buzzing with people, but
the corridors were void, the only sound being the hum of the
lights and the ghostly wind which flowed through the vents.
Perhaps there was a meeting going on somewhere? It wasn't

for a while until Finn came to anything which was noticeably different, and when he did, he was unsure exactly what to make of it. It certainly wasn't like anything he was expecting.

The room behind the grate was wide and contained what looked to Finn like four short, yet deep swimming pools. They were definitely filled with water and had ice crusted around the edges. Whatever they were used for was anyone's guess, but like the other rooms, this one also appeared to be vacant. More importantly, at the other end of the room, close to the usual entrance, was a large metal cabinet of the kind that Finn would often associate with the storage of office utensils. It had one door open and was just begging to be looted.

Well, well! What do we have here? Free stuff just waiting to be stolen? Well, I've already got trespassing and vandalism on my list of felonies, may as well add theft. It's not like any upstanding court is going to arrest me for crimes against literal supervillains who go around kidnapping and shooting at people. They'll probably give me a medal for this.

Getting out of the vents was no more difficult than getting in; all it took was a little bit of elbow grease, and the panel holding the grate in place came off and clattered to the floor. He then he dropped down and took a better look around while he stretched his muscles.

As Finn got a more inclusive look at the rest of the room, he noticed a couple of strange things that he hadn't seen before, like the towel rails situated close to the pools, and the water cooler which was also close by. The towels themselves were especially odd, as they were dripping wet and crumpled, indicating that they had been recently used. Well, if they had been used, Finn wasn't about to hang around to see whoever used them come back, and so he made haste to where the cabinet was and took a peek inside. To Finn's delight, the cabinet was a gold mine. There was a kind of lab coat stashed away in a box at the bottom, and another which held surgical masks and a roll of hair nets. It held everything that he would need to make the perfect disguise… It was such a shame therefore, that the moment had to be ruined by an unknown voice coming from behind him.

'Well, hello there, weirdo. Did you get lost or something?'

The feeling was like having an icicle dropped down the back of his shirt, and despite the context of what was said, it still made all of Finn's hairs stand on end. When he turned around however, there was nobody there. The room was just as empty as before.

'Uh… Who's there?' Finn tested, seeing if the voice would respond.

Silence. There really was not a single soul in the room besides himself, so he checked over the vents, scanned the walls and tried to look into the water in the pools. The water wasn't clear enough to see if anybody was hiding inside, and the temperature made Finn seriously doubt that would be the case. It was only when he turned back to the cabinet and reached for the coat, that the voiced chimed in again.

'You know, it's probably nice and cool up in those vents, but "your sort" don't really need to worry about that, unless you want to catch a cold, that is?'

Finn's eyelid twitched. Someone somewhere in the room, was playing tricks on him. Only talking when he turned away, and spouting complete nonsense whenever he went to do something. Whoever it was, it was a relief that they weren't immediately hostile, but it was still such a bizarre scene. It was easier for him to believe that he had gone insane and that it was just his hallucinations that were talking to him.

Without turning around this time, Finn replied to the voice.

'I just, um... Lost my keys. You know how it is'

Another silence, then the unknown individual piped up again, having apparently come to a conclusion.

'Lost your keys, that's a classic. Oh, the commander is gonna have you put in detention for sure!' the voice snickered.

'Hey! Hey, I don't want to get into any kind of trouble here,' Finn pleaded. 'It was just a simple mistake, could have happened to anyone'

The pauses between their conversation were beginning to play on Finn's nerves. Every time he replied, the other person in the room seemed to be letting him stew for his own amusement. It was infuriating.

'Tell you what, if you can give me something to trade then maybe, just maybe, I might not tell on you. How does that sound?' the voice bargained, slyly.

Finn thought back a while, and after a moment, fished around in his pocket and pulled out the packet of mints that Eric had given him a while back, which were a bit crushed, but otherwise still good to eat.

'Will a packet of mints suffice? I don't have much else on me right now.'

They seemed to be pleased by this offer, as evidenced by the enthusiasm in their reply.

'Oh! Yes, please! You actually managed to get some of those down here? You're a godsend!'

'Okay, but first, I want to just ask a quick question, because I'm a bit lost. Did you see anybody come through here on a stretcher, kind of skinny, wearing a beanie on his head?'

'Yeah sure, he was one of the new arrivals being hauled off to the holding ward for patients after they get "the treatment". He was yelling and screaming; "What the hell! What did you do to me!? I want to go home!", all the way down the hall, poor guy... If you're supposed to be there, you had better get going, they don't like it when people are late around here.'

Finn wanted to go, he really did, but what he heard from the strange person he couldn't see had him rooted to the spot. When it was repeating what Eric had said, it wasn't just his words, it was his voice, imitated perfectly. The sheer terror in every syllable was given to him, word for word, as if from his own mouth, and it was haunting. Still, Finn had got what he needed: a disguise and an objective. He would worry about this strange encounter later; for now, he had to find Eric.

'Hey! Uh... Before you leave, you were going to give me those mints, right?'

Finn was just about to leave with his disguise fully in operation when the request had come again. He was more than a bit disturbed by him, but this mysterious person had helped him, so Finn decided that he would stall for just a moment longer then follow it through.

'Um, okay sure,' he said, and placed them in the middle of the room.

Once everything was ready, Finn was glad to be able to leave that ominous room and advance with his plan to meet with Eric and get him out of this place. The person who had helped Finn watched him leave, until the point where the door swung closed and there was nothing of interest left to see, then a hand, cold and pale, raised up out of the water and snatched the bag of mints, dragging it down into the ice-cold water along with it.

'Wow... What a weird guy...' breathed the voice belonging to a pair of gleaming yellow eyes, which then sunk back under the water.

Finn jogged down the corridor, thinking of things that he could say if he happened to be confronted by anyone, stuff like having urgent business elsewhere, that would work, hopefully. He got to the end of the corridor and found a set of doors which led into a deeper part of the building, they had an imprint with the title: Treatment Facilities. Finn dreaded to think what kind of treatment was employed in this place, but had suspicions that whatever it was, it was bound to be unpleasant. All the more reason to find Eric as soon as he could.

Right then. If I keep going down this way then I should be on track towards this holding ward. Don't worry Eric, I'm on my way!

As a precaution, Finn opened the door a crack and peered through. The room was just as he had feared – a large, open room with lots of people and guards, so he had to take a moment to compose himself and get into character. The trick was going to be looking as though he was in a massive hurry to get to somewhere else in the building. With a deep breath, he stepped in and walked briskly, making his way across the room, towards one of the far doors.

While pacing through the part of the building that Finn assumed was the main part of the treatment facility, he was glad to note that his disguise was working perfectly, and nobody seemed to be taking notice of him. Most of the other people in the room wore a similar outfit to his own and travelled around in groups of two or three, orbiting their tables and pushing papers. Of the guards in the room, most seemed to be lazily standing in various spots around the edges, sometimes breaking off to chat amongst themselves.

Finn was grateful for their lack of alertness; they probably thought that nobody would be simultaneously, both lucky enough to find out where they were hiding and dumb enough to cook up such a hare-brained scheme of infiltration. He didn't stop to take a look at what any of them were doing in depth, and entered through the far door unchallenged.

Phew, that was tense, now to find this ward...

Further along was a set of doors and a window to a room on his left, and another at the far end of the short hallway that he had just entered. He would have raced to the end of it, had it not been for the commotion that was going on inside this other room, which caught his attention. Sneaking a look through the window, he saw something like a cell inside, with bars separating what looked to be a scientist of some sort, and a man in a rather extravagant, military-styled overcoat, who looked to be raving at the one behind the bars. Finn pulled the door open a little, stealthily, and listened in.

'So, what's the problem now? I gave them the treatment you asked for and sent them on their way, I can't gather any more data until after they—'

'Well you're being too damned slow!' the military man barked, to which the man in the lab coat sagged, dejectedly.

'You expect miracles from me and I made them for you. The mortality rate of the serum is as close to zero as it's going to get and I have already made numerous improvements to our end result, anything more than that is going to take time.'

'I gave you time! all the time! Ten years' worth of sitting around and playing with your little experiments, and what do you give me?'

'Exactly what you wanted: the perfect soldiers.'

'What you gave me were a bunch of layabouts who do nothing but sit in their ice baths and skulk about in the shadows feeling sorry for themselves! I asked you for soldiers and you gave me skulkers!' the man shouted, gripping the bars and spitting each word through them. The one who his anger was directed at responded, by simply sitting back in his chair and giving him a smug look.

'And this is the master tactician with his own private army? You want me to just open up their heads and tinker around, so that they'll follow your every command? I call that lazy. Why don't you train them yourself, Maxwell?'

'You are trying my patience, Voe! I have had enough of this conversation, think yourself lucky that you're still of some use to me, or I would have fed you to the incinerator with the rest of the failures long ago!'

That was Finn's cue to leave the immediate area, the last thing he wanted was to be caught in the way of that furious army man, and so he turned away and bolted towards the far door, slipping through and shutting it closed with lightning speed.

Jeez, that was close... Now, where am I?

As it turned out, it was the holding ward, or at least, part of it. The room was like a prison block, two-tiered and with a balcony on either side, with cramped cells lining each of the front and back walls along the stretched, oblong-shaped space. Strangely, most of the cells appeared to be empty. This is where Eric was meant to be, now he just had to get him out of here. There was a clipboard pinned to one of the walls closest to the exit, Finn took it and looked over it quickly to see what it was about. Another success, as it was just what he was looking for, and had a list of names that pointed him to the exact cell that Eric was being kept in, which he raced over to as quickly as he could.

To his massive relief, Eric was there, sitting on a fold-out bed and staring at his feet. They hadn't bothered to change any of his clothes from before he was captured, but by the looks of him, he had obviously been manhandled a bit, although worse than that was his skin. He was deathly pale and shivering. Whoever was responsible for this was going to feel Finn's unbridled wrath once this was all over.

'Oi, Eric! Psst!' Finn called to him, and watched as he raised his head drearily.

'Is somebody there? I'm feeling kind'a ill...'

Finn snapped his fingers to try and get his attention and called out again.

'Come on Eric! It's me, Finn, from work! I've come to get you out of here!'

'Huh... Finn? Finn! Holy hell, is that you? How did you get here!?' Eric questioned him, snapping out of his daze.

'Long story, no time! I'm busting you out of this madhouse right now, okay?'

'You don't have to tell me twice, let's go!' Eric answered, as Finn flipped a lever which caused the bars on his colleague's cell to slide back. In a rush to get up, Eric staggered over to Finn and was caught in his arms. After catching him, Finn was somewhat disgusted by the discovery of some kind of unknown, foamy substance coating his left hand. He grimaced and wiped it off, to find that there was raw flesh around the stubs where his fingers used to be.

'Good lord, what did they do to you, man?' Finn queried, to which Eric looked up at him, straining to keep focus.

'They... put something in my arm... Some kind of drug, I think. I feel really bad, Finn... It feels like everything is going numb...' he slurred.

'Look, stay with me, Eric! I'm gonna get you out of here and get you to a hospital, first thing, but you've got to keep moving!'

In a snap decision, Finn decided that going back through the way he came in would not be the best way to leave, there were simply too many people to run the risk of getting caught. Instead, Finn opted to go down a different route, taking the gamble that it would be a safer choice. Along the way down a corridor similar to the other which Finn had traversed, they had just passed something like a broom closet, when Eric tripped and fell. Distressed by his fall, Finn rushed to pick him up.

'Finn... Please...'

'Come on Eric! I'll carry you if I have to. We need to get out of here!' Finn pleaded.

'No, Finn... Leave me... I'm not worth it...'

'Oh yes you bloody are! You are worth way too much to lose!'

'But Finn... I'm annoying, and a burden on you, I'll just slow you down...'

Taken aback by his words, Finn decided that it was time for a confession.

'Eric... Aw jeez, I'll admit it okay? I was a snarky little scumbag to you at work, and I put my feet up, thinking that nothing was ever going to be my problem, and I took no responsibility. That's in the past now. You are my responsibility and I'm going to make this right, so just hang in there, we should be out of here in... Are you crying?'

Eric was covering his face with his hands and something was dripping from them, something red.

'Finn, I'm... I'm bleeding...'

Pulling his hands away gently, Finn found that Eric's face was gushing blood from his top lip, which had split down the middle and left a tear all the way to the base of his nose, and was continuing to widen while Eric's shaking had amplified. To add a second wave of panic to Finn, the silhouettes of a small group of people suddenly appeared in the doorway of one of the nearby rooms and hastily, Finn was forced to rush Eric into the closet and have him sit down on a box at the other end of the small space.

'Christ almighty, Eric! I don't know what's going on right now, but I'm going to get you through it, alright?' Finn reassured, while he himself jittered with stress.

While Eric could only mumble in response, Finn set about searching, looking for anything that he could use to help him. He floundered, pushing things off of the shelves with reckless abandon. He didn't even know what he was looking for, just something, anything that he could use to stem the bleeding. Finally, he settled on an old cloth, initially hesitating as he doubted the sanitary status of it, then resolving that he didn't have the time. It was when he turned back to Eric that he became much more aware of the severity of this situation.

As Eric reached up with shaking hands, he felt along the edge of the beanie that he was wearing and felt the hair along the outer edge of it curiously, before moving it up and off of his head. To his horror, a large portion of his hair came with it, and the rest was steadily beginning to fall out in uneven patches as well.

'My hair… it's…'

Between talking, Eric's breathing was ragged, and the shaking and bleeding simply wasn't going away. Worse yet, the blood had begun to fizz, turning into the horrible substance that was coating his hand. Finn looked on in sympathy. He had heard of drug trials going wrong and was despairing as his imagination ran wild.

He handed over the cloth to Eric and motioned for him to hold it to his face, while he went back over to the door and turned his back to him in order to check whether the coast was clear. With the door slightly ajar, Finn tried to make his attempts at getting more information on the state of the corridor outside less noticeable by making sure that he wasn't pressed up against the wood as he looked through the crack. He didn't manage to get a very good look, and could only see half of the hallway from his point of view, but the half he did see was deserted.

'Okay Eric, it looks like we could be clear, I'm just going to take a minute to... Eric?' Finn whispered, before he turned slowly to the sound of something cracking, like twigs being snapped at the back of the room. Eric wasn't moving. By the looks of him, it seemed as though he had passed out, but the sounds that were coming from him were a concern: they weren't natural. Stepping over to him, Finn saw that his head was covered by the cloth that he had given him. Tentatively, he reached out to it and pulled the cloth back, unprepared for the horror that he was about to witness.

The sight of Eric's face was ghastly; it was horribly contorted. All his hair was now gone, and as the morbid sounds of snapping and crunching continued, it became blindingly apparent to Finn where it was coming from. The entire shape of his body was changing. His arms and legs were beginning to elongate, with his fingers starting to grow out sharp claws from the places where his fingernails used to be. Likewise with his toes, as an identical set of talons pushed through the material of his shoes. His face completely warped into something else, pulling forwards and merging with his nose, into an alligator-like jaw structure, while his eyes were tightly closed. Finn could only imagine the kind of pain he was going through. As the transformation entered into its final stages, his skin broke into a kind of fast-acting rash, before he was left with a coating of fine, silvery scales in their place. Finn was left speechless. It was so bizarre and sudden that he had no idea how to react, and simply gawked at Eric's slumped, monstrous form.

'Wha... what in the world??' Finn muttered, astonishment strewn across his face.

BANG, BANG, BANG

'I know there's somebody in there! Open up, would ya?'

The terror of being caught couldn't have come at a worse time for Finn. His partner from work, who he had gone to such lengths to save from this place, had just turned into a monstrous, fish-like humanoid, and now he was going to be captured and made to suffer the same fate. Finn's mind was tearing itself to shreds.

'Look, this blood is fresh. We can tell that somebody just went through "the change" in there. Why don't you come out, so we can talk about it?' The voices behind the door continued.

Finn's despair was transforming to anger, now. How could they taunt him like that after something so devastating had just happened? It made Finn's blood boil, and he bunched up his fists. If he was going to go out, he'd do it fighting.

Throwing himself out of the door in a fury, Finn launched himself at the first shape that he could see beyond the door, and instantly regretted it. A trio of abhorrent creatures, all of equal appearance to the thing that Eric had turned into, grappled him by his arms and held him in place.

'Now that was just rude. We only want to help. Your friend in there has been through a lot just now, so he's going to want to know how this all works, won't he?' the creature said while flashing Finn a toothy grin.

The terror that Finn was feeling now was inexplicable. It was like nothing he had ever felt, and his chest was beginning to hurt.

'Don't you go anywhere near him!' Finn shouted as he struggled desperately, but it was clear that while they were advancing towards his friend, Finn was losing his grip on the conscious world, and the pain in his chest stabbed into him, forcing his vision to go black.

CHAPTER ELEVEN

Swimming through the cold, dark seas of the unconscious mind, Eric Jones felt shapeless and strange. He had no control over his body and couldn't feel any part of it, which was different from the last time he'd been forced into a state like this. At least then, he still knew that his body was human, now he wasn't so sure. Something terrible had happened to him, and it had sent him drifting, unable to find himself. In this obscure part of his mind, a voice was calling out, but it was distant, muffled by the low noise which rang in what he assumed were his ears. As the voice got louder, there was another feeling, something that appeared suddenly and made him feel incredibly content. It was unbelievably refreshing, enough to bring him just far enough out of his trance to feel a bit more control, and with it, he reached out…

Eric's eyes snapped open. While blurry at first, his vision eventually cleared, and he was met face to face with a creature who had a head not unlike that of a carnivorous fish. It held a plastic water bottle upside-down in one clawed hand and was pouring it out over him. Suddenly overcome with panic, Eric tried to scream, but the best he could muster was a dull wheeze.

'For Pete's sake, Garth! Give the poor guy some space!' came the voice of a second creature, as the first was pushed out of its way. The second creature loomed over Eric now, yet it kept a more considerate distance than the first, and appeared to be eyeing him with an air of sympathy, or at least as much as could be expressed by a hulking humanoid with the features of a predatory sea creature.

'Poor lad, looks like he's got no idea what's going on right now... We probably scared him half to death, just popping up and looking like this.'

In response, the one known as Garth waved a hand dismissively and took a swig from his bottle.

'He'd have to find out sooner or later. When I found out, yes, I was shocked, but I got used to it, and I'd say that it's better to learn quick than spend the rest of your life jumping at the sight of your own shadow.'

The other one considered this.

'Still, he's just turned, he doesn't even know how to speak yet. We should take things slow with him.'

While they continued to argue amongst themselves, the numbness Eric felt was beginning to subside and he could feel sensations which were alien to him begin to set in. The inside of his mouth felt especially strange. It was longer and had an odd texture on the roof. Not only that, but his tongue could curl back further than normal, sickeningly, to the point where he could probably touch the back of his throat with it. Experimentally, he opened his jaws. And then opened them again.

Now he knew exactly what the ridge along the roof of his mouth was for, it was in fact, the divide between two separate sections. His upper jaws extended outwards and bent back like rubber, making him feel extremely uncomfortable. All three of his jaw sections showed an impressively dangerous set of curved teeth along the inside-edge, which in his upper jaws, would have connected up to where the other would meet, had they not diverged in opposite directions. The new, animalistic fangs that he had acquired in the place of his human teeth felt as though they were practically made to tear flesh from bone. Horrified, Eric commanded the muscles in his jaws to bring them together again and they slotted back neatly.

'See? He's putting the pieces together. He'll be just fine in a day or two,' Garth guessed.

'Well, let's just see how things go for now, we don't want him getting too startled,' the first one commented while watching him.

There was no sense to what Eric was seeing and hearing from these creatures. They looked just like monsters and seemed to have a distinct interest it him, yet, despite his vulnerability, they weren't attacking him. Having dawned on him that he had become something else, having lost the physical aspect of his humanity, he dreaded to think of what he now looked like, and expressed his dismay by trying to procure an answer from the creatures which towered over him. Still, he couldn't utter a word, and any attempt to do so only caused a feeling of strain on his throat.

'Yeah, you're gonna have a little bit of trouble with the whole walking and talking business for a while, we all go through it at the beginning. Why don't we start off with introductions? I'm Theo, and the chap next to me is Garth,' the creature explained.

'That's me... And in case you're wondering just what on earth we are, we're Skulkers.'

The one who had named himself Theo flinched at that description and raised his opinion on the matter.

'Are we? I hate it when they call us that. You know that the guy who runs this place just calls us that to make us feel like trash'

'Is he wrong though? Most of us are a bunch of anti-social gits who don't want anyone to talk to them, or even look at them for that matter, not that I blame them'

That was something that really hit home with Eric. If his body resembled anything like the creatures he had just encountered, then they might be the only people on earth who would tolerate him from now on. He might never be able to go home, to show his face around his family, or even sleep in his old bed. He would be forced to slink about in the shadows as a hermit, too hideous to let anyone see what he had become. The misery was close to unbearable.

'Aw man... Looks like I stepped on a nerve... Sorry about that,' said Garth.

Theo looked to his partner, and then back to Eric, who was still lying on the ground, clearly in distress.

'Let's get him on his feet, he should start to feel a bit better after he's had a chance to get used to it...'

As Eric was helped up, he continued to sob, looking past the tooth-filled maw which extended from his face, and over a body that should have belonged to something out of a nightmare, rather than himself. Every aspect of it felt wrong, even the clothes he wore now weren't his own. It was evident that the other two had decided to redress him while he was unconscious, removing the articles of clothing that had been ruined by his transformation, and replacing them with a garb similar to theirs – a plain T-shirt and a pair of canvas trousers. His hat was more or less the only reminder of his old life that he still had, perched atop his head and damp from being recently washed. It looked out of place on him. His shoes were gone completely and hadn't been replaced with anything, which seemed to be a sensible decision, as the talons that now adorned his bare feet would have torn them to shreds anyway. It was obvious that without the other two to hold him by the shoulders he would simply collapse, while his strength was starting to come back in stages, he was still too weak to support himself on his own.

'Okay, so what we're gonna do is get you over to a bench so that you can rest up a bit more, get you some nice cold water. You're going to want lots of that from now on, and then we'll have a go at seeing if we can get that voice of yours back in action, and you can tell us what's on your mind. Sound good? Nod for yes,' Garth told him, as the two skulkers carried him.

Eric sniffed and nodded his head, feeling resigned to his fate. It didn't take long for the pair of skulkers to escort Eric to a table, and when they arrived, they sat him down and both took up a seat opposite him. It appeared that the room where they were situated was something resembling a mess hall, including the tables, benches, a plethora of water coolers and a serving counter. There were no windows, so Eric couldn't tell how deep within the building they were. There were a handful of humans working in the kitchen beyond the counter and one manning the counter itself, none of whom seemed to be at all bothered by the alien appearances of the ones they were serving.

While Eric was staring into the palms of his hands with tears streaming down his face, too upset to care that both hands once again had a total of five fingers, Theo mentioned to Garth that he would leave the two of them together while he would go up to the counter to check the menu, before bringing back meals for the three of them. In the meantime, Garth tried to make small talk with him, somewhat unsuccessfully. When Theo returned, he placed down a large tray with three plates of food, and a fourth which held an assortment of fruit.

'I wasn't sure what he would like, so I just picked up a bit of everything,' said Theo, happily.

'Really? They don't usually let us do that. Well, we had better make the most of it then,' Garth replied, plucking a grape from the fruit platter, and then turning his attention to Eric.

'Hey, new guy. Lemme show you a cool trick.'

Garth curled his right hand into a fist and balanced the grape on top of his thumb, before flicking it up into the air and catching it between his front fangs. The first part of the trick was simple enough, with a little bit of skill a human could easily do the same. What would be nigh impossible for a human however, was when Garth turned his head to the side and showed the grape being passed along the tips of his teeth like a conveyor belt.

'Yep, we all have teeth that can do that as well, it's probably one of the weirder things about us. That and "chirping",' Theo said, while Garth used his tongue to unhook the grape from a tooth that it was skewered on before swallowing it whole.

'I had almost forgot about that, we'll have to teach him how to do that too, after he gets his voice back, of course. Oh, and one other thing, just after we found you, there was another guy who you were with. We don't know his name yet, but we sent Natalie off to get him some help... We haven't heard back from her yet, but we're keeping our fingers crossed.'

Garth snorted.

'Yeah, Fingers crossed. I've got all the confidence that she'll get him the help he needs, but still... Natalie is kind of a dork,' he stated, to an unimpressed stare from his friend.

'I'll tell her that when she gets back, you know. She would probably claw your face off,' Theo replied, earning him only a cocky grin from the other.

'Not a problem, I'll just grow a new one.'

Eric was still upset, but having been reminded that Finn was still involved in what was going on was enough to break him out of his self-pity, and he tried to communicate to them that he wanted to know more. Talking wasn't going to work, so he settled for trying to sign it to them, and uneasily, the two of them shared a look, then spoke up.

'Look, we, uh… We really weren't expecting it to happen but after he came bursting out of that closet and charged at the three of us, we… we may have given him…'

'… A heart attack'

Finn's eyes were half-lidded, and he felt utterly terrible. Somebody was trying to talk to him, but the lights were just too bright, he wanted to go back to sleep.

'I'm telling you that what you suffered was a heart attack. Now wake up! You have answers to give me!'

Finn squinted, and as he started to slowly wake up, he suddenly felt something clasp firmly around his face. Jolted by the sudden presence of danger, he regained focus and found himself to be sitting down, restrained to a wooden chair in a small clinic, with a rather furious-looking man in a medical mask, squeezing his face with one hand and holding a scalpel close to his neck with the other. While his focus was most immediately placed on the man who was threatening his life, it was also apparent that there was another entity in the room. Standing in one corner was a tall, scaled creature, with its arms behind its back and a kind of muzzle secured around its jaws. It was staring at the both of them, and it seemed to be just as confused as he was.

'Oh, you've noticed "it" have you? It's no wonder you had that heart attack. If it was my first time seeing them, I would be scared out of my skin too.' The doctor spoke, while making his way over to it.

'That is of course, until you realise just how utterly useless they are! All day, every day, they just mill about, eating their way through our resources and giving nothing back! It's like we're running a free-range farm here!' he exclaimed loudly, to which the creature glared at him and made a sound like a rattlesnake.

'Ugh... What the hell is it that you want?' Finn asked, while he struggled in his seat.

'What do I want? How about for starters, telling me how you got in here, you cockroach!'

Looking down, Finn found that his disguise was no longer effective; only the padded factory worker's uniform remained.

'Damnit, look, I can explain what this is about. I came here looking for a friend. I just want to find him and leave, nothing else—'

'Is that it? You just happened to stumble into our facility, that we've spent the last ten years in, being cooped up underground, cut off from the outside world?' The doctor interrupted, twitching slightly as he paced up and down the room.

'Uh... Pretty much,' Finn hazarded as his answer.

There was a moment of silence before the doctor walked back over to Finn's chair and set the scalpel down on a table beside him.

'Absolute moron... The kinds of blithering incompetence that I have to put up with on a daily basis is staggering...

Can't even keep the common filth from breaking in now? This place is falling apart...' He muttered under his breath in between short bursts of cursing, before returning to Finn with a calmer demeanor.

'I think that right now, it would be as good a time as any to just wind down and relieve some stress...' The doctor spoke, ominously.

'... But first, some trivia, since it appears that you are unaccustomed to the habits and traits of our skulkers.'

The doctor pointed at the creature mockingly.

'These abominations are the work of Andrew Voe, a miserable waste of human skin who spends all day, tinkering in his little cage and giggling about how great he is. These vermin are what he makes for a living. He calls them his "pride and joy". Disgusting, truly disgusting creatures'

Again, the rattling noise came from the creature, but it was quickly silenced when it noticed what the doctor had just picked up from the table beside Finn.

'Perhaps the only thing that I happen to like about them is that they have excellent healing properties, so no matter how many parts you slice off of them, they'll all grow back over time. Heat however, is a different matter, oh, it'll heal just the same, but these skulkers have such a high internal temperature thanks to it, that a little extra heat, and they melt from the inside-out'

What the hell is this guy going to do? He's lost the plot!

There was a different look in the eyes of the monster now, while before they were bright and defiant, now it looked terrified, and as the doctor approached, the tension only escalated. Finally, the doctor stopped inches away from it and raised what was in his hand at an angle where Finn could easily see it. It was a blowtorch.

'After I'm done, I'm going to let my superiors know of this breach in our security, and then... Well, they can decide what they want to do with you,' he said, before lighting the pilot on the blowtorch and turning to the cornered and helpless creature.

While the attention of the doctor in the room was focused away from him, Finn made his plan for escape, and rocked back and forth in his chair. As Finn struggled, the room soon became engulfed in pained screeching, coming from the corner of the room. While the sounds of torture went on, Finn was getting closer to his goal, the scalpel was nearly off the table, and with one last strong jolt, it tipped off and fell into his hand.

Bingo! Alright, you looney, get ready for some hurt!

The scalpel was sharp and not exactly designed for cutting through the straps which were securing his arms, but it did the job, and with one cut free, he could easily undo the other. Totally engrossed in the act of burning into the helpless creature's shoulder, the doctor was completely oblivious to the fact that his other captive was now free, and also levelling the chair that he had previously been fastened to, over his head.

'Does it hurt!? I bet you're wishing that you were still human, you wretched piece of—'

Smash!

The chair came down on him, so hard that it split into two pieces, and the doctor dropped like a log. Finn stood there for a while and breathed heavily, holding half the destroyed chair in his hands, before throwing it away and regaining his composure. The creature, which the doctor had called a "skulker", backed away until it reached the wall, and then leant against it, while it stared at Finn with a mix of surprise and relief.

'Honestly, I don't want to think I just killed a man, but if I have, I'd say that I'm probably doing the world a favour,' Finn said to the alien creature, regardless of knowing whether it could understand him or not.

Looking over the body of the man who Finn had just bludgeoned, he decided that he would double down on the assault and battery by looting his pockets as well, and found a handful of keys and a card with the man's photograph. Turning back to the other entity in the room, he found it to be in pain, and was looking at him pleadingly.

'Alright, easy. I'm going to come over and unlock you. Just don't go biting my head off, agreed?'

The creature nodded eagerly, his first sign that it could understand him, or at least the first that he could remember. There were hazy memories from just before his heart attack. Had he really encountered these creatures before?

Getting close to it, Finn saw just how bad the damage from being burned could affect one of these creatures. The area affected by the burn was roughly the size of a softball and around it, the scales were starting to turn black as they began to dry out and fall off as flakes. The inner area was much worse however, and showed pink flesh which was bubbling, and even the beginnings of bone, as the creature's body was starting to degenerate. As soon as he opened the handcuffs from behind the creature's back, it squirmed desperately and shoved past him, dashing over to another part of the room and disappearing behind a medical curtain.

Soon, Finn could hear the sound of running water, and presumed that it had gone to tend to itself. Curiosity taking somewhat of a dangerous leap over his own person safety, Finn decided that he wanted to see what was going on, and took a look through a gap in the screen. There was a lot of splashing going on, the creature was pressed up to a water cooler at the back of the room and madly shoveling water from the cooler's nozzle onto its shoulder, hissing through its muzzle as it did. After a short while, the creature seemed to become enraged and ripped the tank off of the top of the cooler, and held it above itself as the water drained out over it.

Okay, Finn... You've really got yourself in over your head this time. You've just set free a seven-foot-tall fish-monster, that may or may not want to kill you and eat you. Are you absolutely sure that you'd like to roll for diplomacy?

While Finn was still making up his mind, there was an echoing thud as the empty plastic tank of the water cooler fell to the tiled floor and bounced once, before rolling away. With the source of water in the room all used up, the creature's searing yellow eyes were now focused on Finn, who was feeling ever more uncomfortable. It was now easy to see just how large and menacing it was, as it slowly stepped out from behind the curtain. Finn could feel the hairs stand up on the back of his neck when it began to reach behind its head and tug at the straps which connected the muzzle to its face, and with the mask unfastened, the creature tossed it aside and began to approach him. When it reached Finn, who was frozen in place, too terrified to move, he could clearly make out every gruesome detail which identified what it was that stood before him, something unlike any living being that he had encountered before: the creature's claws which could tear him to shreds in a heartbeat, its inhuman yellow eyes, and its jaws which capable of snapping Finn's bones like twigs. Despite possessing a wound which would have been the death of an average person, which stank badly and now seemed to be producing some kind of foam, the creature would still be more than capable of killing him. As his terror reached its peak, the creature bent down and wrapped its arms around him.

A moment passed, and in this moment, Finn felt like he was in freefall. He fully expected the monster to begin crushing him into a smooth, Finn-flavoured paste at any moment, but it just held him there. More than the constant fear, its injury carried a noxious odour and was starting to make him feel very nauseous, and this was helped in no part by the heat that was coming off of the creature itself. It was like being hugged by a bony and foul-smelling radiator. With the acid rising in his stomach, he would have to protest.

'Please let go of me, I'm gonna be sick!' Finn whimpered from under the creature's embrace.

Immediately the creature released him, much to Finn's surprise, and after a moment of hesitation, he raced over to the nearest waste paper basket, which was tucked under the doctor's desk, and relieved himself of his lunch. When Finn next raised his head to see what the creature was doing, he found it to be standing by itself, looking at the floor and wringing its hands.

'I'm sorry for doing that… I just don't know what came over me,' it said quietly, while looking like a dog who had just been told off.

The confusion was headache-inducing. The man interrogating Finn had claimed in his sadistic ranting, that skulkers were originally humans, but for such an outlandish notion to be true was something that he wasn't quite ready to accept.

'What? So, you can talk now? What in the world is going on here?!' Finn demanded, still baffled by the creature's sentience.

'I don't know! You just saved me from being burned alive, and I was so relieved, I didn't know what else to do!' The creature blustered awkwardly.

'I mean, why am I in this room? What happened?' Finn asked, hoping to clarify the situation.

Guiltily, the creature responded 'You're... you're here because I took you here after you blacked out. I thought that you were one of the other doctors, so I just did what I was supposed to do. I had no idea that this was going to happen... This is all my fault...' it sulked.

'Oh, for the love of... Look, I don't know what you are, or where you came from, but I don't want to be involved in whatever is going on here, I'm only here to rescue someone. If you know where he is, just tell me, so I can find him and leave.'

The creature seemed to acknowledge this and faced him properly now.

'I know where he might be. He's the one who you were with just before you blacked out, right?'

'Who else?' Finn answered sarcastically.

'He should still be with a few friends of mine. I'm sure that he's well looked after, but... I have to take you a long way to get here. The lounge is on the other end of the facility.'

Finn wasn't sure exactly how far that would be, but he suspected that it would be a long way, considering how big the place had looked from the outside. He only hoped that he would be able to figure out this mess before somebody with more dangerous intentions found out what he was planning.

'Alright,' Finn said as he got up from the floor 'Right now, all that matters is that I find him before something else happens, so I should leave as soon as possible.'

'Absolutely, I'll lead the way! Whatever happens now, I'm going to make sure that you're repaid for what you've done for me, you have my word!' it exclaimed, much to Finn's displeasure.

'No. You're not leading me anywhere. Just tell me what way to go, I don't want any more meetings like this or any other craziness going on! I have had my full share of crazy for today, I'm not having any more!' he ranted, while getting up and heading for the door.

As the skulker began to protest, and moved to make an attempt to stop Finn from leaving, they both heard a clattering sound behind them and saw that the doctor, who they had previously thought was knocked out, was getting up and scrambling along the floor, until he found his old scalpel and pointed it at them accusingly.

'If only... Ack! If only that heart attack had killed you!' he spluttered, struggling to keep himself upright as the blood matted into his hair and trailing down onto his lab coat showed just how injured he was.

'When my superiors hear of this, they'll send every guard in this building to catch you! And when they do, they're going to bring you back to me! And I will get to enjoy flaying you alive!'

Unfortunately for the doctor, his madness was cut short, when in a split second, the skulker appeared in front of him, eyes burning with hatred, and a clawed hand raised above his head. In one cruel motion, five sharp claws cleaved through the air and raked down on the doctor, shredding through his lab coat as if it were made of paper, and left five jagged lines from the top of his forehead, all the way down to his navel. It was over in an instant, and he collapsed onto the floor with barely a flinch. Afterwards, the creature shivered and looked back at Finn tentatively, knowing that there was still blood dripping from its talons.

'Mister...?'

Finn backed away from the skulker, his face awash with terror. It had killed a man. There was a moment of hesitation when it had started talking and acting like a human, but now there was no denying it. To him, this creature was a terror in the night, a real-life monster with a hunger for blood, and one wrong move would leave him just like that – slashed up and bleeding out on the floor. He had to get away and save himself, somehow...

'Don't... don't come any closer...' Finn stuttered.

The creature looked at him curiously. Through Finn's lens of paranoia, it looked as though it could be eyeing him up as prey.

'I didn't want to do it, but at least he can't hurt us now,' the skulker breathed, and wiped its bloodied hand on some papers that the doctor was keeping on his desk.

Looking down at the corpse in the room, he could tell that he was definitely dead. He had lost so much blood that there was no way he could possibly be alive. This was the first time that Finn had seen a corpse up close, and to be so close to the one responsible for it was unthinkable... Yet perhaps something that he could use to his advantage, if only for a moment.

'It's dead, is it? Look again! It looks like he's getting up!' he yelled.

Franticly, the skulker jumped into action, readying itself to attack again, but was confused to find that the doctor was still on the ground, unmoving.

'It's alright! He's not moving, but why would you- Hey! Wait!' It called out as Finn took the chance to leave the room as fast as he could, hoping to put some distance between himself and the murderous skulker, long enough to find a hiding place. Regrettably, this night had turned from a rescue operation into yet another fight for his life.

CHAPTER TWELVE

Crashing through the door, Finn nearly collided with another one of the monsters. They were everywhere, this was their hive and he had just disturbed it. As he scrambled to a running pace, he could feel the eyes of every one of them in the hallway fixed on him. He was still weak from earlier, having survived impossible odds for the second time, but still pushed himself to continue, as chatter regarding his sudden appearance broke loose. This of course, turned into more concerned arguing amongst themselves, when he rammed into one of the human lab workers who tried to stop him. He had come this far and wasn't about to just give up and let himself be killed, especially with death so close behind him… He was going to make this creature run a marathon if it wanted to take his life. Looking back, Finn could see the skulker that he had set free start to give chase, pleading with him to stop running as it did.

Nuh-uh! Nope! I'm not falling for these lies, not after what it just did. I need to get away and hide somewhere, and when it's gone, then I can worry about getting out of here!

He shoved his way through a set of doors, down a flight of steps, and through a doorway to an area that presented itself with bright red warning signs and a placard which read: "AUTHORIZED PERSONNEL ONLY". Well, that wasn't going to stop a man running for his life. He only hoped that it would be enough to deter the monster that was hot on his trail. Upon entering this new area, Finn was startled by the lack of light. The room was pitch black and ominously spacious, as alluded to by the echo that reverberated when he slammed the door closed behind him. This would be his hiding place. He had no idea where he would go, but in somewhere as large as this, there was bound to be a place that would offer enough cover to keep him out of sight, but he would have to find it fast, as he was losing his strength to stand.

Running towards the centre of the room, Finn was almost startled out of his skin when he was met with a wall. It was impossible to see anything in front of him, but at least he could use this new surface to feel his way around. Thankfully, he had got out of that hallway fast enough that he had time to find a place before the skulker would find him, but there was something about this room that unsettled him. It wasn't as dead quiet as he had expected it to be, in fact, it was fairly active, there was breathing all around him. Feeling around this wall a bit more as he made his way along it and deeper into the room, he found that the flat, cold concrete intermittently was replaced with metal bars, that he assumed were there to act as a holding cell.

What is this? Another prison?

At the end of the room where he had come in from, the door was opening, so if he didn't pick up the pace, he would be found, and that would be the end of him. Deeper into the room he went. He could hear it approaching now. The monster was calling out to him. It might have terrified him even more than his encounter with the home invaders now, with them, his only fear was a quick death from being shot. With this however, he was bound to be torn limb from limb.

Petrified with fear, Finn reached into his pockets, searching for something to calm his nerves, something that always worked when he was stressed out. His fingers managed to detect it, deep within the confines of his pocket, and under the veil of darkness cast over the room, he brought it up to eye level, feeling it over to tell which end he needed to light. At that point, Finn had assumed that he was far enough into the room as to not be noticed by his pursuer, at least until it would give up and leave, and fished his lighter out.

The lighter was flicked once, then twice. He usually didn't fail to get it working very often, but his hands were shaking, and it was a struggle to see anything in the dark. Three times now, and still no flame. Finn laid his back up against one of the barred walls, this was starting to get irritating. On the fourth time, the lighter's flame flickered into life, and he cupped his hands, shielding it from view. After getting his cigarette lit, he rested for a moment and kept his ears open for any signs of danger. The monster's voice was getting more and more distant, but there was no doubt that it was still searching for him.

crcrcrcrcrcr

The sound sent a shiver up Finn's back, it was right behind him. The only time before where he had heard such a sound was in the office of that crazed doctor, while he was strapped in and helpless. This clicking, rattling noise, was a warning, akin to something that an animal would make when it felt threatened.

CRCRCRCRCRCRCR

He could feel hot, pungent breath on the back of his neck, now. Whatever was behind the bars was close enough to reach through and touch him. This was not a safe place to be.

It's nothing to be afraid of… If it talks like the other one, maybe it can be reasoned with… Just turn around slowly…

Carefully, Finn moved his back away from the bars and peered behind him. There was definitely the predatory face of a skulker behind the bars, staring back at him menacingly, however, it wasn't quite the same as the other one that he had encountered before. Knowing full well that it was probably a bad idea, Finn moved his hand which held the lighter closer to the caged creature, and saw just what it was that separated it from the other in terms of appearance. It was quadrupedal and crept low to the ground like a dog, and its face was contorted into a hideous snarling visage. If this creature had ever been human before, there was no trace of it now.

Perhaps sensing the lighter's flame coming closer to it, the creature reacted viciously by snapping and hissing at Finn loudly. This in turn seemed to set off the other ones in the adjacent cages, and soon the whole room had erupted into a cacophony of blood-curdling shrieks and rattling fangs. The cigarette dropped out of Finn's mouth, and his whole world shut down.

Eric discovered that getting a grip on his life again was slow-going and arduous. While he could perform most actions now without need of assistance, learning to speak again was a matter of learning how to use something which was completely alien, yet still a part of him, just as much as the claws, and the teeth, and the jaws that split open. As he continued to practice under the watchful eye of the resident skulkers, Theo and Garth, it was obvious that he was struggling.

'So, as I say, it's going to take a while to get used to it, so there's really no need to feel like you need to rush yourself,' Theo reassured him, while showing Eric around some of the lounge's features.

After hearing of Finn's heart attack soon after Eric was revived inside the facility's mess hall, he had been distraught and was causing a scene that was starting to distract the other residents from their meals, and so the two of them thought it best to escort him to somewhere that would be more comfortable for him to gather his bearings and adapt to his new life. Adapting was not something that Eric was keen on accepting however; he was in denial that this was a future he would have to endure, and as he was toured around the lounge, with its wet floors, soaked furniture and judging occupants, it was quite obvious that he didn't want to even entertain the idea that this would be his new home for the foreseeable future.

'Fffiii...nnn?' Eric strained while he looked to his mentors for support.

'Don't worry about it, pal, Natalie's got that covered. She knows where to find us, so I'm sure everything is going to be alright,' Garth said, while offering him a paper cup filled with water from a nearby cooler. 'Have a sip, you'll feel better.'

There was a feeling of uncertainty when it came to being given something from someone who until quite recently had been a total stranger, and even more so from somebody who would look more at home stalking boats in a distant bayou somewhere. The liquid inside the cup was clear and didn't smell of anything suspicious, although both Theo and Garth were watching him as if expecting something extraordinary to happen.

'Hey, no need for that look. It's not like we would poison a new friend. Drink up, while it's still ice cold,' Garth encouraged while pushing the cup into what used to be his hands.

'Don't try and force him, Garth. Let him have it if he wants it,' Theo interjected.

'Pssh, fine. But I'm starting to feel a little dry, myself, so I'm having one. It's only water anyway.'

After filling a cup of his own, nearly to the brim, Garth tilted his head back and drank roughly half of the water before he stopped and tipped the rest over the top of his head, spilling some of it onto the ground as he did.

'Good stuff, that is. You've gotta keep your moisture levels up, otherwise you get all flakey and nasty. It's just another one of the perks we have to live with.'

That wasn't something that Eric considered to be a very pleasant fact about life as a skulker, but as far as unpleasantries went, it was tamer than he had expected. Rationalising that they had shown him that they wouldn't intentionally try to cause him harm, and that they knew more about living in this place than he did, he brought the cup to his mouth and took a couple sips. Surprisingly, for only being a cup of plain ice water, it felt a lot better than he had expected, almost exactly how he had felt just before waking up to his new life. Intrigued, he pulled the cup away and examined it carefully, as if yielding it to reveal some kind of hidden secret. The other two chuckled, and Garth made a gesture to Eric with his empty cup, showing him a tipping motion. It seemed obvious what he wanted Eric to do, but it just seemed too out-of-place to him. It wasn't something that he would normally do when he was still a human being, doing something so silly would be quite pointless and would only result in him looking like a fool and having to change his cold, wet clothes. Still, he wasn't human anymore, and it was something that Garth had done, knowing that it was something that their species normally did. Maybe it would make him feel better?

Tentatively, Eric raised the cup, still with a little water in it over his head, and glanced at his instructors briefly, who were both giving him a thumbs up, before he closed his eyes and tipped.

Feeling the cold water splash over him, running over the ridge of his jaws and down the back of his neck, into his clothes, he opened his eyes, and then blinked. From just a bit of water, he was left with a feeling, like basking in the light of the first sunshine you get after a terrible winter. It was sublime, but also felt strangely normal to him, like this would just be something that he did all the time. What came after however was a disconcerting feeling, and a guilty, self-loathing, that he was starting to normalise these kinds of experiences. It made him think of home, his real home, and want it even more.

'So, how do you feel?' Theo asked. 'Did that do the trick?'

Eric looked at him and sighed.

'Yes... It was good. I want to go home though, is there any chance of that?'

Garth pointed and seemed to be pleased about something, but curbed his enthusiasm after sharing a glance with Theo and a wordless conversation between the two of them.

'Well, it's good to hear that you've got your voice back, I did think that a bit of water would help. but that is really sad. I'm sorry, but there's no leaving here, nobody gets out.'

'Nobody at all?' Eric asked in a disheartened voice.

'Nobody,' Garth answered back. 'Nobody gets in either, not that I would imagine they would want to, this place is completely—'

'Finn got in!' Eric cut in abruptly.

The two skulkers paused for a moment at Eric's interruption, as they mulled over what he had said.

'Finn did what? This is that doctor you were with, who we're talking about?'

'He's... Actually, this might not be the best thing to tell you out loud. He's not a doctor, he's my mentor at where I work... Where I used to work. I don't know how he got in, but he'll have a way out, I know it.'

Theo and Garth stood and looked stunned. While he knew that relying on Finn to have a plan of escape was a long shot, especially if getting in had been as much of a fluke as he could expect, Eric still had faith that he would be the one to get him out. If he could convince some of the other people here to help him, that would boost Eric's chance to escape tremendously. He just had to pray that whatever the plan was, it would be one that would work.

'You're pulling our legs, aren't you?' Garth accused Eric, suspiciously.

Eric flailed in response.

'No, I'm not! He'll tell you himself when he gets back to us!'

The two skulkers looked to each other and Garth tilted his head.

'It might be true though. It hasn't happened before, but maybe?' Theo pondered.

'Hah. Maybe. Or maybe he's still just a little bit woozy from the change and talking a load of cuck-oo,' Garth commented.

'I'm not! What reason do I have to lie to you!?' Eric pleaded, before he began the wheeze, having over-exerted his voice box.

'Hey there, take it easy, we didn't mean to tease you. It's just that we... Hold on. Something's going on outside,' Theo said, noticing that the other skulkers in the room were congregating by the windows at the far end of the room.

As the three rushed over to see what was going on, they stopped for a moment to ask some of the others what they had missed.

'There was something big going on outside. I haven't seen this happen before,' one of them said.

'There were trucks heading out of the building in a hurry, some kind of commotion up on the surface, maybe?' came the voice of another.

Eric looked through the window to see that there was indeed, a lot of activity moving away from the facility, to the far end of the cavern.

'Where are they going?' Eric asked Theo.

'The exit, I presume. But it's not like any of us could get out that way even if we tried. There's a massive door up there that only ever gets opened when they deliver new people to get changed. What these guards are doing now is a mystery.'

Eric continued to watch along with the rest of the lounge's occupants and wondered where these events had placed him.

Deeper inside the building, a lone figure, and someone who had just returned from the surface, made his way quietly to a solitary door set within one of the building's inner walls and let himself in. When he was inside, he turned to face a familiar set of bars, with a dishevelled-looking man in a scientist's lab coat, standing with a proud look upon his face.

'Every time... I can't believe the risks that you're taking. This is all going far too quickly,' the visitor said to him, visibly panicked.

'Is it? I would say that the plan is right on schedule, and as far as risks go, none of the suspicion is on us. Things couldn't be going better.'

'What I mean is that… You know what I'm risking, Mr Voe; what planting those documents have done, the kind of repercussions it could have… I'm having second thoughts…'

'Dear me… After all you've done to help, you're having second thoughts now? Is that true, Mr Barnsley?' Andrew asked.

'I am… And I did. Two people are already in danger because of me. Despite my warning, one of them is already—'

'I know, he was here. It's already done,' the doctor interrupted, confirming his fears.

The visitor looked ashamed. This was becoming a very bad day for him.

'In any case, my informants tell me that there has been a rather surprising development. Somebody broke in, and I have a sneaking suspicion just who it was…' Andrew Voe chimed, teasingly.

'It wouldn't be Finn, would it? How would he even do it?'

Andrew's grin was nothing short of worrying.

'Who knows. He got in though, and Adams is losing his mind over it. He thinks he's brought back-up outside, so he's diverting his mercenaries, the fool. That gives us ample time to get the plan underway.'

Josh Barnsely had been shocked to see how many guards were patrolling when he had arrived at the building, thankfully who didn't suspect him, but knowing this was the result of Andrew Voe choosing today as the day to unleash his plan was giving him shivers.

'I know that we both want to leave Maxwell's shadow for good, but I'm just not sure that I'm ready,' Josh admitted.

'Hmm… Well, I have someone I'd like you to meet. You're going to like this, he's been waiting to see you all day,' Andrew said in an unusually happy voice, as he walked to the rear end of his cell and reached into one of the noisy cages. 'This is Mr Lilac. Adorable, isn't he? I named him after an old friend… One who I wish was still here to see the fruits of his brilliance.' The doctor cradled a white, fuzzy animal with long, floppy ears in his arms.

'Um… I am quite fond of rabbits,' Josh admitted.

'And don't you think he'll make just the most adorable little hybrid?' the doctor cooed, still smiling as warmly as ever.

'You didn't seriously…' Josh muttered.

'I may have given him a little dose,' the doctor continued, and turned the rabbit around so that it was facing him.

'Are you going to rip Maxwell's face off, Mr Lilac? Are you? Yes, you are,' he said to the rabbit in a childlike voice, all the while grinning like a cat.

The rabbit simply stared back at him with its beady little eyes and wrinkled its nose.

Having known Andrew for a couple of years, Josh Barnsley knew that over the course of his incarceration, Doctor Andrew Voe's mental health had been tested by the moral ambiguity of the actions which he had been corralled to perform on the countless victims that Maxwell Adams and his hirelings had abducted to fuel the mercenary leader's ambitions. But each time that the cracks started to show, he couldn't help but feel sorry for the man.

'The plan isn't seriously going to involve using a killer rabbit to assassinate Maxwell, I know that,' Josh assumed.

'Of course not,' Andrew replied honestly. 'The kind of fate that I have in store for Maxwell will make him wish that he could have a thousand killer rabbits instead… All in due time…'

Deciding that he had spent enough time with the doctor, the visitor bid him farewell and closed the door behind him, leaving Andrew once again, alone in his cell. Watching him leave from the window beyond the bars, Andrew sighed and set the rabbit down on an office chair next to him.

'He knows what the plan is, and he knows that no matter what happens, there will be bloodshed. Maybe he will choose to stay by my side after this has all come and gone. It would be a lot safer for him that way. What do you think, Mr Lilac?'

A few drops of blood were starting to drip from the animal's nose and it was quivering.

'Oh yes, you're a rabbit. Silly me. I guess I'll just brood over it until the time comes,' the doctor said, and smiled as the changes began to take place.

CHAPTER THIRTEEN

Have I died and gone to hell?? I don't know how much more of this I can take! The petrified inner thoughts of Finn Lacksley cried out and bounced around the cracking eggshell of his mind.

The sound coming from every corner of the room he was in was like the wailing and shrieking of some kind of abominable zoo, and having met his wit's end, Finn's only response was to curl up in defence, covering the sides of his head in a desperate attempt to drown out the noise.

I... I just can't take this... My damned heart is going to give out again! I knew that this was far too dangerous and stupid to do on my own, but I made myself come here anyway, why did I—

Something grabbed him from behind. This was it. His life was over. Any minute now, he would feel those razor-sharp teeth bite down on him, ending his life in a horrible, gruesome way. But first, he felt the grip of the creature pulling him up and onto his feet. Then it began to make him walk, obviously wanting to move him somewhere more secluded before tucking into its meal. As he walked, the sound of the enraged skulker-like animals began to fade away until it was faint by comparison to where he was now. He didn't dare open his eyes, too afraid of what he would see to even contemplate getting a look at his surroundings. He could tell that he had exited that dark and hellish prison and had been taken down a few corridors before he was forced to stop. Only after having made it far enough away, did the one who was directing him decide to speak.

'I'm sorry... I'm so sorry that you had to go through that. I need to be more careful, otherwise somebody could come along and... and...'

Finn recognised the voice: it was the same skulker who had murdered a man right in front of him. It sounded close to tears.

'I messed up... I was only trying to protect you and I messed everything up.'

Even if the creature was a vicious murderer, it sounded miserable, and while he was still terribly afraid of it, just listening to it feeling sorry for itself was starting to get embarrassing.

I might die down here but, just for once, I need to man up and take a stand! There will be a way out of this, I just need to make one. Do something! Just do anything and get away from it!

He began to feel delirious.

Finn's lighter was still clenched in his hand, and having seen the kind of effect that fire had on them, he knew that this would be what he needed to drive it away. Pushing his fears aside, he stared the creature down and raised the lighter to its face, successfully lighting it on the first attempt. There was an awkward few seconds where neither one of them did anything, and Finn just stood there, trying to look intimidating while the jitters were making his arm wobble. Judging by the injury, which had shrunk significantly since their last meeting, it could heal itself quickly enough that burning it would be the only way for him to truly make any sort of impact, however, without much effort, the skulker took a small breath and blew the flame out.

Great idea, moron. You tried to threaten it with a pocket lighter, what did you think was going to happen?

'Look… We really got off on the wrong foot. Can we talk about this? Please?' it asked.

Finn lowered his arm, having embarrassed himself long enough. If there was no way out other than to talk his way out of this, he would have to make the decision that it was better than nothing.

'Um, okay… Hello, I'm Finn, nice to meet you?' he ambled, offering the terrifying monstrosity in front of him a weak-willed handshake and the smile of someone who really didn't want to be in this position. His inner monologue determined that such a display was frankly quite pathetic of him, and he cursed himself for having said it, but after hesitating only for a moment, the pale creature accepted it and clasped its warm hand around his.

'I'm Natalie… And again, I'm so sorry about this.'

Judging by his expression, Finn was having some trouble wrapping his head around the skulker's introduction of herself.

Natalie? This thing is a Natalie!? The first introduction I get to one of these "skulkers", who look like something that crawled out of Creature from the Black Lagoon, but with more teeth, who kills a man moments after I meet them, and its name is Natalie!?

'Um… Finn? Are you going to be alright? I know that I look scary, but I want to help you, if you'll let me?'

'I-I have no idea what is going on anymore…' Finn admitted. 'I just want to get out of this alive, is that too much to ask?'

Something moved at the other end of the hall, causing both of them to panic for a moment, but it seemed as though it wasn't anything that would put them in danger, and it passed without noticing them, but having been made aware that the area was still active, Natalie chose to take Finn by the arm and persuade him into moving again.

'What's going to happen now? Where are we going?' He asked as she dragged him along.

While trying to help him keep up the pace, Natalie answered; 'Some friends of mine are looking after your friend. If we meet up with them, then the five of us might be able to find a way for us to all get out of here. You managed to break in, after all.'

It was troubling that Finn had spent this long in the building and hadn't yet come up with a solution on how to leave yet, and more so that Eric was left in the care of total strangers, and worse yet that they were skulkers. There would be no way to know anything about any factor of his situation until the time he got there, and that was the biggest problem of all. Not knowing what to do in advance made his every move wrought with risks that could come from anywhere.

'Can I get some idea of what's going on here? I get that there is some kind of freaky experiment going on down here, but there's still a lot that I don't know!' Finn asked, hoping deep down that the answer wouldn't be as dreadful as he feared it would be.

Natalie slowed down a bit so that they could catch their breath, then answered him.

'When there's enough time to spare, I will try to explain as much as I can, but as long as we're inside then there's a chance that we could get caught...'

Outside, searchlights on the roof of the building followed the trail of last few mercenaries who had been ordered to leave for the surface under the rumours that a full-scale raid could be taking place any minute, and with the lack of communication between them due to his choice of locale, their leader who was watching them go would be cut off from them until they had put a stop to what was going on. The mercenary leader turned away from the edge of the roof with his face furrowed into a scowl.

'Everything was meant to be contained, orderly and under control. I have lookouts and guards stationed all over the place, and now? Now everything is falling into chaos because somehow, one little data breach causes the whole operation to go up in flames! This was meant to be a closed environment, nothing gets in, nothing gets out, and now both has happened and I'm boxed in like a rat in a cage!' the leader angrily vented.

There was a number of other personnel on the roof with him, who regarded him with the same caution as they would a rampaging bull. Having learned from experience, and knowing that Maxwell Adams had kept his position of leader by maintaining a tyrannical presence over the rest of them, they knew the kind of backlash that would come from invoking his ire, especially when he was in a bad mood. Maxwell pointed at two of them and beckoned them forwards.

'You, and you, form by me! We're going to take a trip down to where our doctor is keeping his horrible skulkers occupied, and if they refuse to talk, we'll torch them one by one until they spill their guts on who this intruder is and where we can find him. As for the rest of you, man your posts! Do not make me ask twice!'

Obediently, the mercenaries took up positions, with the two that would be accompanying him flanking him on either side. Each one of them were equipped with a specialized suit, made to protect them from the heat produced by their weapons, a pair of portable flamethrowers.

The three of them stomped into the building with the intent to get an answer for their trouble, either that or to end up with a lot of fried skulkers to scrape off the floor afterwards, and boarded the lift that would take them down to the building's lounge. Standing inside of the elevator and waiting to arrive at his destination, the mercenary leader stirred impatiently.

'He's playing tricks on me... I know this is his doing. Andrew Voe and his circus freaks. I gave him everything that he wanted, barring freedom, and this is how he shows respect? I'll kill him when I get my hands on him again... But not before I turn this intruder into a lump of charcoal first,' he muttered.

When the three of them had reached the first floor and the doors slid open, their leader took position in front and exited first. At the end of the hall, he spotted two shapes dart across a junction, one dragging the other behind it, and both heading in the direction of the lounge. Maxwell's eyes narrowed into a sneer.

'There you are. I hope you two are up for some exterminating, because we have a rat to fry!'

Close to exhaustion, Finn felt as though he was on the verge of collapsing by the time he and his newfound ally burst through the door to the skulker's lounge. The other occupants cast glances at them, but none were quite as shocked as Eric and the remainder of Natalie's companions, who rushed over to pull them into a quiet corner of the room. Garth was the first out of them to speak up.

'Oh my God, Nat, you're injured! What the hell happened?' he gasped, losing the sarcasm for a tone of genuine concern.

'Nothing!' She blurted out, before withdrawing slightly, having realized that she had raised her voice.

'I mean... n-n-nothing serious... It's really Finn that we should be worrying about.'

All eyes were on Finn now, who was being supported by the shoulders. He was panting heavily, but raised his head to look over the skulkers who he was being introduced to. One of them stood out to him much more than the others.

Eric Jones stared at the man who he respected as his former mentor from behind the set of ghastly jaws that adorned his face. His eyes began to water.

'Finn...' he wheezed as the words caught in his throat.

Having determined that this was indeed the person he was looking for, wearing the same hat that he recognised from earlier, yet irrevocably changed, Finn gave him a weak smile in response.

'Good to see you again, Eric... Did I ever tell you about what an awful weekend I've been having?' he asked, half-jokingly.

It was a wonder how Eric could still cry after having done so much of it already; his tear ducts felt dry, but when his emotions took over there was no stopping them. Finn Lacksley, the workplace mentor who had bullied him with his snide comments and lack of empathy, wasn't anyone who Eric thought that he would cry over, but after risking his life in his attempt to rescue him and nearly losing it in the process, he had more than a reason to do so now.

'You did... It has been pretty awful, hasn't it?' he replied, unaware that as far as how awful their weekend had been, it was about to get a whole lot worse.

The door to the lounge swung back violently and a total of three humans entered through the doorframe, dropping the room's ambient chatter into complete silence. At the sight of them, the skulkers in the room moved to cover themselves behind tables and other furniture, fearing the glow from the pilot lights of the devices they carried. The one in the middle scanned the room with a look of disgust, turning to one of mirth when he found what he was looking for.

'Don't any of you move an inch, unless you want to end up cooked!' he boomed at the five.

Keeping his bodyguards close by his side, the mercenary leader waltzed across the room and spun Finn around to face him, then pulled him up by his collar and glared into his eyes furiously. When Finn's companions rose to come to his aid, he barked at them to back off, and his bodyguards levelled their weapons threateningly. When the man was convinced that Finn was sufficiently terrified, he dropped him and spat onto the floor.

'What a miserable wretch you are. And here I was expecting this threat to be something substantial, but it turns out that you're just some puke-stinking loser who got in on a fluke!' Maxwell bellowed. 'But I would like to know, what your plan was, if you even had one at all. Come on, entertain me,' he taunted.

It was hard for him to regain his nerves after being shaken up so badly, but Finn forced himself. It was that, or die.

'I don't have a plan…' Finn admitted, which only served to prompt the mercenary into sharing a look with one of his guards, bearing ominous intent. 'Really, I just broke in to help a friend. I've been making everything up as I go along!'

The leader waited a moment before asking vaguely, 'Positively?'

Finn shuddered.

'Yes… Positively…'

The leader of the three mercenaries looked like he was struggling to keep a straight face, mere moments before he burst out laughing.

'Oh, ha-ha! That cracks me up!'

Suddenly however, he was back to a more sinister expression, exuding malice with every word. 'Cretins like you are too worthless to waste good ammunition on, but I think that an example needs to be made, especially so that the rest of you rejects will learn to do as your told from now on!' he bellowed, taking a revolver out from a holster on the inside of his jacket.

The first to respond was Natalie, who put herself between Finn and the gun-wielding brute.

'If you want to get to him, then you're going to have to go through me!' Natalie challenged, taking up an aggressive stance and splitting her jaws to show just how many teeth would be coming his way if he decided to attack first. This earned her a curious look from the man, and he pointed the gun towards her clawed hands.

'You've got some blood on you, missy. Do you have a confession to make?'

Natalie didn't take her eyes off of him, but pulled her top jaws together so that she could respond.

'I don't know what you're talking abou—'

'Oh, I think you do!'

In the next instant, the gun was pointed directly between the defiant skulker's eyes. Not a single creature in the room stirred.

'One of my lab coats was found, face down, in a pool of his own blood not too long ago. He was killed by one of you skulkers!'

Behind the two who were being confronted, Theo and Garth pulled close and whispered to each other.

'Nat's killed someone? What the hell?'

'That isn't like her. She… she wouldn't do something like that out of choice… Would she?'

Theo clasped a hand over Garth's snout angrily.

'No. She wouldn't, so don't even think like that, or I swear to God, I'll—'

'Hey, you two back there! Do you have a death wish?'

The threat had come from Maxwell Adams, who now had his handgun directed at the both of them, while one of his bodyguards was keeping the nozzle of his flamethrower pointed at Natalie and Finn.

'Uh… No sir, don't mind us,' they responded in unison.

After the interruption was quelled, the barrel of the gun returned to point at Natalie's abdomen and the leader of the three mercenaries started up again, but this time with a smirk on his face, having thought of something that would be suitably evil to appease his morbid sense of humour.

'So, you've killed once… How would you like to do it again?' He asked, and awaited her response.

When she didn't answer, the grin slipped slightly from Maxwell's face, but remained intact as he continued without her.

'You see that miserable waste of human skin, cowering behind you?'

Natalie turned her head slowly, just enough so that she could see Finn, who hadn't moved from the spot. He looked scared.

'Kill him.'

CHAPTER FOURTEEN

Dread permeated the room like a foul odour, pouring off of the occupants as they waited in anticipation. For Finn, the fact of the matter was that he was going to die, either by the hands of Maxwell Adams and his mercenaries, or by Natalie, the skulker who he was just beginning to trust. His eyes wavered to her taloned hands, and followed the bloody smear that ran along the underside of each claw, and he wondered if would he end up like the mad doctor who she had slashed open? The mere thought of it sent shivers down his spine, but while he contemplated his fate, it was becoming clear that Maxwell was getting impatient.

'How about I rephrase that for you! Would you like to see what happens when a room full of skulkers gets hit by two streams of burning propane?!' he yelled at her.

A fearful, chittering sound could be heard from deeper in the room after he issued this threat. Natalie had been given an ultimatum, either kill an innocent man, who had risked his life to rescue his friend, and who had saved her from being tortured, or be responsible for the horrific deaths of nearly everyone in the lounge. Natalie was shaking.

'I… I won't do it! You're insane!'

Maxwell raised his free hand in a signal to one of his bodyguards, who turned to the watching crowd. The watchers sunk a little further back, trying to hide behind anything that they could.

'Words of an expendable resource...' Maxwell commented. '...You skulkers are here because I need an army that can stand up to the might of the world's nations, but when the operation that we are conducting here is finished, they won't be skulkers like you, they will be my perfect, un-killable soldiers! Until I get them, all of you are expendable!'

The other skulkers in the room were fixated on the sight of the flamethrower's nozzle. Skulkers were extremely vulnerable to heat, even having their clothes catch fire was enough to leave them close to death, and Natalie had only survived by dousing herself in enough water to cool her injury, the scales on her shoulder were still blackened and caked in blood-foam. If a skulker was to be hit with something as hot as flamethrower fuel, they would be considered lucky to instantly liquefy. All the pressure was now on Natalie to make her choice.

'I'm going to give you until the count of three, after that, these fish are getting smoked!'

Natalie returned her attention to Maxwell and clicked her teeth threateningly at him.

'One...'

She looked at the crowd, catching sight of the fear in their eyes.

'Two...'

She looked back at Finn again, and behind him she saw the face of Eric, who was open-mouthed in shock.

'Two and a half...'

She made up her mind, and raised her claws to strike.

'I'm sorry Finn!' Natalie cried, and Finn squeezed his eyes shut.

When nothing happened, Finn looked at what was in front of him and breathed heavily. Natalie's claws were an inch away from his throat, but her eyes were streaming with tears.

'I-I can't do it...' She wept, and then turned around angrily. 'Do you hear me?! I said, I won't do it, and I meant it!'

For a moment, the leader of the mercenaries was taken aback, but quickly recovered and huffed an annoyed breath.

'Alright, fine by me,' he said nonchalantly, and then shot her in the stomach.

Natalie fell backward from the force of the blow, and the others were quick in trying to rush to her aid, but were stopped when one of the flamethrower-wielding bodyguards stepped in to motion them a warning.

'Come on now... I know that it takes more than that to kill one of you freaks. Don't you want to be a hero? One last chance?' he taunted.

Natalie spluttered and coughed up a handful of blood, which quickly began to fizz as it dripped onto the floor.

'Go... hurk... Go to hell.'

Maxwell's patience had met its limit now, and with that, he gave the order to his bodyguards, who now aimed both nozzles at the crowd.

'Torch 'em.'

click *click*

As the mercenary leader watched, his smug expression dropped into one of total confusion, made even more relevant by the visible panic that his bodyguards were now experiencing.

clickclickclickclickclick

'Well? What the hell are you waiting for!? Get on with it!' their leader shouted at them.

Having come to the discovery that the weapons of Maxwell's minions weren't going to function, the denizens of the lounge began to rise from behind their makeshift barricades and carefully advance towards them, but not before one final visitor to the skulker's lounge had made his appearance, who was immediately recognised by everyone in the room... Especially by Maxwell, whose face turned into a visage of pure rage.

'You...' he seethed at the man who had just stepped in.

'Yes, me. Oh dear... You don't look very happy to see me, not very happy at all.'

The man was dressed in the same kind of lab coat that was donned by most of the other laboratory workers in the building, although his hair was noticeably unkempt, having only been hastily trimmed. There was an odd creature perched on his shoulder, which glared at the mercenaries as its owner fully entered the room. It looked to be some form of skulker-hybrid, and was the size of a small cat.

'You insubordinate scum! What the hell do you think you're doing out of your cage?'

The doctor tapped a finger on his chin mockingly and then shrugged.

'Staging a little coup d'état, which trust me, has been a long time coming.' He chuckled at the enraged military man.

When Maxwell began to raise his revolver to fire at the doctor, in a heartbeat, the entire room was on him, and he only managed to get a few shots off into the crowd before he and his bodyguards were wrestled to the ground and the gun was wrenched from his grip. When he had finished surveying the leader of the mercenaries to ensure that he was properly restrained, the new arrival sauntered over to Finn and his companions.

'Well, this could have gone a lot better. You have my utmost apologies, Natalie Boman.'

The stricken skulker looked up at the man standing over her. She was too absorbed in the effort of staying alive to comment, but knew what his presence meant.

'And as for you, Mr Lacksley, I believe that we haven't been properly introduced. Doctor Andrew Voe. I owe a lot to you today.'

Between the wild coincidences and death-defying luck that he had encountered, Finn was astonished to have defied the odds, and now be face-to-face with the man who had orchestrated everything that had happened as of late. All of the secrecy, all of the kidnappings, the underground laboratory and the soldiers protecting it, it was all to hide him and his creations from the world until they were ready to be unleashed. But when he looked at the doctor, there was only one thing on his mind.

'So, you're the one that's been turning people into monsters down here, yeah?'

The doctor looked hurt for a moment.

'I wouldn't call them monsters, to me they are as far from that as could be. To answer your question though, yes. The serum that I have concocted is of my making. What results from it is what you see before you,' Andrew answered.

Finn gestured to Eric, who was helping to tend to Natalie, along with Theo and Garth.

'When we get out of here, he is going to be leaving as a normal person, do you understand?'

Andrew looked over to Eric, taking notice of his regrown fingers and his more noticeable non-human appearance, and pondered on what to say.

'I usually don't make promises, but I will say that when we leave this place behind, I will do everything within my power to ensure that he will be normal.'

From the moment that he was pinned to the floor, all throughout their conversation, Maxwell had been screaming profanities at the group. By comparison, his bodyguards had already given up on fighting back, and when the doctor returned his attention to the mercenaries, he had Maxwell's guards separated from him, and their leader was forced to stand.

'You're a dead man, Voe! You'll never leave this place alive!' he ranted.

Andrew merely waved his threats aside and reached down to pick his revolver up from the floor.

'So, all this, and you're just going to shoot me? Do your worst.'

The doctor inspected the gun, taking his time and testing the weight of it before passing a cursory glance over the helpless mercenary.

'Dear Maxwell...' the doctor spoke. 'I would only use this if I had changed my mind and decided to offer you any mercy. Over the years that you have kept me trapped here in this wretched prison, you've done more than enough to convince me that you're completely undeserving'

With his speech made, Andrew handed the revolver over to Finn, who took it hesitantly. He could have chosen any one of his skulkers to hand the gun to, but the gun had been given to him. The metal part of the barrel was still hot, and the stigma of what he could potentially do with it was making his hairs stand on end.

'What the hell...? I really hope you're not expecting me to use this.'

'Only if it becomes a last resort. You would do well to stay armed down here, especially while undertaking this task that I have for you...' the doctor explained, and as he did, he took a piece of paper out of an inside pocket on his lab coat and unfolded it.

'This is a map of the complex.'

There was a space on Andrew's map that was marked with a bright X, which he pointed to and described the route to get to it.

'Located here in Maxwell's office is an item of great importance to me. Now that I have done a favour for you, I will need you to return the favour and retrieve this for me.'

There was an air of unease about how this request sounded to Finn. In truth, he just wanted the day to be over, but on the other hand, he would surely be dead if not for the doctor's intervention. There was also still an underlying side of him that hated the doctor for what he did to Eric.

'I... Okay, but this is the last thing that I'm doing down here, when I get this for you, I want to see you sticking to your word. What am I looking for?'

The doors to the lounge closed shut as Finn made his way down the hall in the direction of Maxwell's office. Eric had decided to go with him to ensure that Finn stayed safe, but was concerned over his haste to do what was asked of him so unquestioningly. There was something wrong, and Eric was determined to get to the bottom of it.

'Finn... Are you alright?' the newly turned skulker asked his mentor.

It looked as though Finn was ignoring him, although his stony expression showed that it was more from a reluctance to answer him than any kind of malice. He had his head facing forwards and looked to be deep in concentration on the task at hand, but after a while, he spoke up.

'I don't know what to bloody say, Eric. I won't be alright until you're out of here and cured.'

When Eric looked at Finn, he could sense the kind of guilt that he was going through, and wanted to at least make an attempt to sympathize with him.

'You know, it's not your fault... All this—'

'Bloody hell, Eric! Of course, it is!' the man burst out, startling his companion.

'If I had got to you just a moment sooner, then you would still be... You'd be...'

Finn looked to be on the verge of a breakdown.

'I was there. I saw you get carried off into this damned building and I just stood there like a lemon and watched it happen!'

It was painful to hear how Finn had blamed himself for what had happened, but Eric had gone along with him on this task partly because he wanted to reassure him.

'But you came in to get me out! You risked getting killed for me... It doesn't matter what I look like, what matters is that we both get out of here alive!'

There was a lengthy pause, in which Finn seemed to calm down, although he still bore a worried look on his face. Eric swallowed. It wasn't something that he was used to, having Finn worry over him like this, he was more used to being berated and told that he had done something wrong. Seeing Finn feel guilty about him seemed like an extreme reaction, coming from him.

'Eric... What do you think your dad's going to think if we get out of here and he sees you like this?' Finn questioned.

Eric wasn't entirely unprepared for this question, but it still had a solid impact on him. He had practiced for this, and feigned a smile, trying to show that he wasn't bothered, despite how much the question really did bother him.

'I'll deal with that when the time comes,' he answered, to which Finn turned his glance to the floor and huffed.

'No. You're getting cured. Even if I have to beat seven kinds of hell out of that doctor, you're leaving here a human being, or I'll die trying.'

Andrew fidgeted. He had been through his phase of pondering on the morality of his decisions, and should have been solely focused on the monumental task of rallying his former test subjects into a force that would be able to overwhelm the remainder of Maxwell's hired guns while they were currently divided, but looking back on Maxwell himself, and seeing him in this vulnerable state had him torn between his responsibilities and the thought of getting payback for all that he had done. Making up his mind on the matter, he decided that he would take the time to ensure that the mercenary leader got his just desserts, and casually strolled up to him.

'So, how do you like my skulkers now, Max?' He laughed, positively dripping with charisma.

The restrained mercenary leader gritted his teeth and glared at the doctor.

'Do you really think that they belong to you, Voe? You only got to make that serum because I was kind enough to lend you all of that poor, dead friend of yours's paperwork. You're nothing but a fraud!' Maxwell spat.

Deep within his memory, Andrew Voe could still remember the final moments of Doctor Harvey Lilac after he had been forcefully administered a dose of the prototype skulker serum that had been crudely assembled by the mercenary leader's arctic research team. From a glass window, he was made to watch his respected colleague fail to properly assimilate the concoction and be reduced to a pitiful lump of boiling flesh. His strangled cries for mercy had rung out in his dreams that night, and every night after until he realised the true potential of the serum. It was then that he saw the meaning behind his work, and vowed to see it through to the end.

'Did you know that whenever Harvey did research on a subject, he liked to leave little quotes, just off the top of his head?'

The man snorted in response.

'Should I care? If he really wanted to share his "little quotes" so badly, he should have done a better job at staying alive. '

Andrew's eyes narrowed. The temptation to lash out at him was strong, but his desire to draw this out was greater. This would be his piece de resistance when it came to his final interaction with Maxwell Adams. Nothing was going to take this away.

'I have taken a number of Harvey's quotes to heart, but the most precious to me has always been this: "Humanity craves advancement, but sometimes you need to take a step back to realize how far you've come".'

On completing his statement, Andrew reached into his inside pocket for a second time, and pulled out a small metal case. Upon opening the case, a misty vapour escaped from the box, and from within it, the doctor drew out a syringe containing a dull red liquid. The sight of it sent Maxwell into a cold sweat.

'Of course, it's not an exact replica of the treatment that poor Harvey received, for what little good that it served him, even that shoddy piece of work had a mild anaesthetic.

I was wondering what would happen if I simply removed the anaesthetic element of the prototype serum altogether,' the doctor explained as his sadistic side began to spread its wings.

Looking at the syringe floating delicately in the doctor's hands, Maxwell's panic turned into a spiralling void, with only one last catch to set his mind at ease, before he was dragged down into utter despair.

'You don't have your chair, doctor... Do you think that you can frighten me with that, when you're not even using it right!?'

Hearing this, Andrew beamed mercilessly and brought the syringe to Maxwell's neck, while the skulkers holding him down tightened their grip and watched with delight at what was about to happen.

'Maxwell Adams, my dear friend... I never needed it to begin with. Now, this might sting a little... From what I recall, the symptoms begin to manifest sooner and the actual process is much slower, But look on the bright side, this is your ticket to a front-row seat, to see just how much I have improved'

The needle slipped in under his skin.

'No refunds.'

CHAPTER FIFTEEN

Some time had passed, and as Finn and Eric rounded a corner on the lead up to Maxwell's office, they began to see the corridors becoming more decorative and opulent. Walls that were framed with pictures and trophies of the mercenary leader's past victories, many of them picturing him posing triumphantly alongside his hired goons in front of war-torn landscapes, passed them on the lead up to their destination. The door to the office itself was unlike any of the others in the building, being constructed from solid wood and intricately carved, and after testing the handle, the pair found it to be locked tight. Eric looked at the door, then at Finn, anxiously.

'Um... Should we go back and see if that guy had the key?' he asked Finn, and then started to panic as Finn took out the revolver he had been given and aimed it at the lock.

'Wait, wait, wait! What if the bullet bounces off it and comes flying back at us?'

'Eh?' Finn answered in a confused tone. 'That sounds like the kind of stuff that only happens in video games. Just relax, I know what I'm doing.'

Moments later, there was a small chunk blown out of the door, and the recoil had catapulted the gun out of Finn's hands, launching it several steps behind them. Finn's flinch was delayed by several seconds, then he shook off his stunned look and approached the door to cautiously give it another try, with none of the spectacular results that he had hoped for. It felt as though the impact of the bullet had caused some stress on the door's support, but even after hefting his weight into it, Finn found that he didn't have enough strength to force it open.

Something squeaked, it was apparent to Finn that it wasn't the door, as he had ceased interacting with it. After hearing the sound again, he turned to find that the sound was coming from Eric, whose hands were clasped tight over his mouth. His pupils had also dilated and the ivory hide on his cheeks had turned to a brighter colour, in contrast to the rest of his bone-white scales. The change in Eric's state had prompted several reactions for Finn to choose from, but the most immediate were brought on out of fear. What if this was another reaction, like when Eric had initially changed into a skulker? He had to make sure that this wasn't the case.

'Are you alright there, Eric? Don't tell me that you're going to change again.' Finn sounded genuinely worried.

Eric was still squeaking, but he tried to talk through it, despite having some difficulty.

'I'm… pff… I'm sorry… I can't…' he struggled.

Upon releasing his grip, Eric threw his head back and laughed, causing Finn's expression to go from fearful and anxious, to bewildered by the change in the atmosphere of the situation.

'Oh God… Your face! Ha-ha! "I know what I'm doing", and then it flies right out of your hands!' Eric chuckled, oblivious of how he had used Finn's voice while making an impression of him.

Having been alleviated of his concerns, Finn pinched the bridge of his nose and despite his embarrassment, found himself joining in.

'Okay, maybe I don't always know what I'm doing... Aw man, I thought I was gonna have another heart attack.'

When the two of them had settled down, they set their sights on the door again, looking to formulate a new plan of entry. After mulling over his options, Finn decided to make a suggestion.

'So, Eric, are you feeling strong?' he asked, innocuously.

'Kind of... I mean, I don't know if I've got any stronger after what happened'

While going back to retrieve the revolver, Finn gestured to the door.

'I would say that shot I put into it has weakened the door a bit. Give it a bit of elbow grease and it'll probably come off the hinges,' he stated.

Eric looked over the door judgingly, and having sized it up, took a stretch and backed up to get a running start.

'Alright, here goes.'

From Finn's perspective, it was quite impressive to see Eric build up speed and cannon into the door using all of his strength. The door was ripped out of the frame from the first blow and tipped onto the floor heavily, splintering some of the broken wood onto the patterned carpet of the room beyond. Inside, the two were greeted by an interior that was lavished with marble podiums containing the spoils of the mercenary leader's exploits – walls with in-built aquariums swimming with schools of exotic fish and a desk that presented itself regally as the centrepiece of the room, holding the obligatory gold-plated globe and a large bottle of vintage wine upon it. Truly no expense was spared when it came to the living conditions of the would-be world conquering tyrant that was Maxwell Adams.

As Eric entered into the room, rubbing on the spot where he had bashed the door down, Finn strolled past him with a whimsical skip, and pulled the bottle of wine off its rest to give it an appraisal.

'So... is it any good?' Eric asked curiously, joining his partner at the desk.

Finn scanned the label and retrieved a pair of glasses and a bottle opener from a nearby compartment.

'Hell if I know, I'm giving it a try anyway. Do you want a glass?'

Eric winced and shook his head.

'Erk... No thanks, I don't really drink wine. Too posh for my tastes.'

Uncorking the bottle, Finn poured out a glass and then waited until Eric was distracted by something else in the room, before he took a swig of it straight from the bottle.

Unfortunately, Finn wasn't able to stop himself from alerting Eric, when the wine turned out not to be especially palatable by his own tastes either, and resulted in him spraying a mouthful of the bottle's contents onto the carpet.

'Augh... This stuff tastes like cat's... No, wait...'

He stood for a short while and analysed the taste that was left over with a faraway look, before going back to his statement.

'It actually has quite a pleasant aftertaste,' Finn commented.

Eric seemed to be quite amused by Finn's conclusion.

'So, You're keeping that, I take it?'

Finn wedged the cork into the bottle's head and put it back down on its rest, then tutted, giving the thought of taking it with him it's due consideration, before finally slotting his index and middle finger under the base of the rest and levering them both off of the table. The wine bottle hit the floor, broke off at the neck, and spilled out onto the carpet, causing the rest of the wine to gush out from the broken container.

'Whoops.'

Eric watched the carpet soak up the remains of the liquid as he continued to wander around.

'Um… That was kind of wasteful…' Eric sighed.

Joining Finn at the desk, the two of them started to root through the drawers in search of the mystery object that Finn was tasked with finding. It was when Finn spotted a small catch at the bottom of the last drawer, that Finn began to perk up.

'Bingo. Let's get a look at this thing, I won't be handing it over if it turns out to be anything dangerous…'

Pulling on the catch caused the floor of the drawer to detach and reveal a secret compartment underneath, containing a small metal case. Finn took the case and stashed it into his back packet, satisfied that he had got what he needed.

'Alright, we're done here. Walk in the park,' he exclaimed joyfully.

The operation that Maxwell had shipped from the icy wastelands of the arctic all the way down to a quiet, rural neighbourhood in the United Kingdom, was meant to be a walk in the park. The mercenary leader had assumed this, and now he was struggling to walk at all. His body was covered with wounds that he had sustained while making his escape from the clutches of his former prisoner, which now began to froth and build up foam on his ruined uniform. Spluttering and choking, he brought a hand to the place on his neck where the needle had pierced him and then took it away, to watch as the fresh blood on his hand reacted with the air and turned into a sticky mass of bubbles that only skulkers produced. Something shifted its position within his ribcage, causing him to stagger and grit his teeth until the pain had passed, and when it did, his eyelids snapped open, bloodshot and filled with fury.

'How... how dare he do this to me!' he yelled through the pain.

Despite the protest from his aching limbs, Maxwell forced himself to walk. During his escape he had caused quite a scene, somehow gathering the strength to wrest himself from the doctor's patients and fight his way out of the room, pummelling the creatures that got in his way in a feat of strength that he knew no human should have been able to accomplish.

Upon recognising that he was changing, the ones that had followed him out of the room had slowed to match his pace. A small group of skulkers, no more than five of them, followed Maxwell's trail, keeping themselves at a safe distance. It was a fair assumption to make that doctor Voe had passed on some of his knowledge on the early tests to his followers. They knew that the burst of strength he had experienced was temporary, lasting only as the assimilation of his body's cells started to take hold, but when the test failed, as it often did, the enhanced cells would become malignant, attacking healthy cells and destroying his body from the inside out. Maxwell shuddered at the thought of becoming one of the doctor's experiments, but even more so at the possibility of being reduced to the sad, abominable state that Maxwell's prototype test subjects were left in. Whatever his fate would be, whether he was doomed to suffer as Doctor Lilac had, or find a way to cut his own life short, saving himself from the gruesome end that the doctor had planned for him, he knew that without any anaesthetic, his last moments would be spent in agony.

Another internal component painfully dislodged itself, forcing the ruined man to the floor, where he heaved until it had settled into a new position. Clutching his abdomen, Maxwell glanced back, and could see his pursuers pointing and laughing. This was a joke to them, seeing him in this vulnerable state and taking delight in his torment. It made his blood boil, which may have been happening literally as well as figuratively. Trying to pick himself up, he found that there was more happening to him now than the mutant blood and the rearranging of his organs. His hands, the muscles within them and even the bone at the centre, were starting to go soft, and bent in a hideous fashion when he tried to lift his weight. It started as pins-and-needles, then grew more intense as the sensation crawled up his extremities towards his centre of mass.

'Ha-ha! look at him flop around, he's like a fish out of water!' One of the following skulkers heckled.

'Aww, poor guy!' Another commented. 'He's gonna be wanting a lot of water pretty soon… Too bad he's not getting any!'

The skulkers jeered and made imitations of him from the other end of the hall, poking fun at his floundering form and stalking him as they got closer. As he gathered up what little willpower he had left, Maxwell pressed his weight onto the doorway to the next corridor, and with enough exertion from his jelly-like limbs, he opened it and slipped through. Curiously, while he was losing control of his arms, he had still retained most of his strength, he simply couldn't use it on anything, with bones that had gone limp and useless.

Spotting a grate close to the floor, Maxwell decided to exploit this opportunity to lose his pursuers before they had a chance to torment him any further, and pulled his body up to it. By this point, the softening had spread up his throat and entered his mouth, where it made the inside seem to collapse. He opened his mouth and spat out his tongue before he had a chance to choke on it, and then coughed hoarsely. The only part of his body that would follow his commands now was his back, and only enough to force him to sit upright. Despair began to set in as he found that tearing off the grate would take more power than he could muster and he started to cry, half in pain, and half from knowing that everything that he had built up in life was being taken away from him. He lamented that he had been stripped of his right to see the world fall under his control and sit on the top, as the most powerful man alive. Instead, he was going to die in a labyrinthine laboratory, inside of a dingy cave, miles underground, as a pathetic shell of his former self.

Spasms started to pulse from within him now, the most unbearable of which wracked his head, making him thrash and yell, and just when he thought that it couldn't get any worse, the skin around his cheeks began to pull to either side, forcing his mouth to widen. The effect was excruciating, and he knew what came next. Just when he felt his face reach its breaking point, his upper lip tore open and he let out a scream. Shuddering after his face had been so horribly mutilated by the transformation, it was time for the next phase to take effect, and from behind his disfigured lips, the bones in his mouth began to grow.

Yellow eyes peered through the gap in the door's frame, looking to catch a glimpse of their prey, before they pushed it open and scanned the hallway beyond, and when looking further towards the end of the hallway proved unsuccessful, the collection of skulkers shuffled their way in.

'Did any of you see where he went? He couldn't have just, up and vanished!' the leader of the group questioned to the others.

The other members looked around frantically, until one of them caught sight of the trail of blood that Maxwell was producing, which led into a ventilation duct and disappeared around a bend within the wall. Next to it was the vent's cover, which was splattered with the same substance that had formed his trail. Upon closer inspection from one of the group, they found the grate to have been crushed as it was being pulled from the wall, and in the process, an object had become lodged between the grate's metal plates. The skulker doing the investigating pinched the object between his claws and pried it free, revealing it to be a sharp, curved tooth.

'Hey, boss. Take a look at this, would you?' the skulker said, handing the tooth over to the leader.

The leader took it from the one who was crouched down by the vent and held it up to the light. He then turned to one of the other members of the group and showed it to them, cracking a wide grin so that the others could compare the shape of it to his own teeth.

'Oh, he's really turning now… It won't be long before he's a pile of mush! Let's catch him before he goes all the way, I want to see his face when it happens.' One of them chimed enthusiastically, while another gave their leader a mischievous grin and piped up.

'His teeth are setting in now… That one is even bigger than yours. Do you think that they'll get so big that they poke through his brain and kill him?'

The leader laughed and flicked away the lost tooth.

'Who knows... But we had better find him soon. The show is about to start.'

The whole group turned when a stricken, groaning sound emitted from the vent, and they stalked over to it to get a better listen. The sound echoed out of the opening and into the hallway, where it met the ears of the skulkers. Each one of them had been through experiences with the leader of the mercenaries, none of them pleasant, which was why they had elected to track him down and ensure that he would not be coming back to bother the doctor while he was planning his breakout, and hearing him suffer was music to their ears.

'Where does this vent lead, again?' one asked.

'It goes into the mess hall. If he's made his way inside, maybe we could grab a snack before he kicks the bucket?' another responded.

The leader patted the one kneeling by the vent on the back and whispered close to his earhole.

'Not you though, Charlie.'

The inspecting skulker looked up at him, seeming disappointed.

'What? Why not me? I want to be there when he gets his just desserts, as much as any of you,' he protested.

'That's because you'll be guarding this side in case he crawls back the other way,' the leader explained.

Charlie, the skulker who had been chosen to stay behind, relaxed, having understood their intentions.

'Yeah, that does make sense... Heh, and if he does come back, I'll have him all to myself!'

Forming back together, the skulkers left for the mess hall, and as they got further away from the vent, the sounds coming out of it turned less and less human before they abruptly stopped. Moments later, there was another entirely different sound, which slunk out of the cold, metal passageway. One that if the group of skulkers had heard, they would know better than to peruse. Charlie, unfortunately did not have this sense of danger, and sought to get a closer look at where it was coming from.

...crcrcrCRCRCRcrcrcr...

He poked his head into the vent upon hearing the sound, and swivelled around the first corner, hoping to catch a glimpse of the target.

'Starting to feel a little "different" are we, Max?' He chuckled to himself. 'The others have gone the other side, so there's no use trying to escape. Why don't you crawl back to me? I promise, I'll make it quick...'

The rattling, tooth-clicking sound returned again, but this time, it was joined by the sound of straining metal and heavy movements, until their origin seemed to be mere millimetres away. Feeling confident, the venturing skulker pulled his head back from the vent and shouted down the hall.

'Hey guys! I found him! Are you going to come and help, or what?'

Although, it appeared that his companions had already left. Shaking his head, he dipped back inside.

Peering closely into the darkness of the cramped ventilation shaft, he caught sight of something poking out from the far end of the vent, and in a mixed bid of impatience and excitement, he stalked closer to it, before launching himself around the bend with his claws primed in a predatory stance...

CHAPTER SIXTEEN

Having retrieved the doctor's "object of interest", the two interlopers, Finn and Eric, had begun to journey back towards the lounge in the knowledge that their ordeals within the building would be over soon. While they walked, Eric began to notice that Finn wasn't keeping pace as well as him, and stopped him to ask what the matter was.

Finn sighed and rested his back up against a wall.

'I'm feeling a bit tired, that's all,' he explained. 'We shouldn't be stopping, if it's not serious enough to be life or death, then I'll just tough it out.'

Eric scratched the back of his neck, feeling bad for the man.

'No, come on, Finn, you've been sticking your neck out for me way too much lately. When was the last time you ate something?' the skulker queried.

Put in an uncomfortable spot by the question, Finn grimaced. He never much liked other people inquiring about his decision-making. It made him feel like he was being talked to like a child.

'I don't see why it's any of your business, I've gone without food for longer than this and I was fine afterwards. It's no big deal,' he stated, dismissively.

Yes, this was definitely the old Finn Lacksley. Eric was starting to get used to the idea that his workplace mentor had been replaced with a more charismatic and likable Finn than the one he knew on the surface, but this was exactly like him, unnecessarily obtuse and even a little hostile at times. He was going to be stubborn and not let him lend a hand if it was the last thing he did, and by the look of him, Eric could guess that there was every chance he would pass out from exhaustion before making it back to the lounge. Rubbing his face, Finn pushed himself off of the wall that he was slumped on and continued his trek in the same, sleepwalking motion that he had been showing for the last few minutes, joined by Eric, who crept behind him.

'There's a place where we could get some food, not far from here... It's actually on the way back—'

'Eric, I said no,' Finn grumbled, deliberately trying not to raise his voice. 'Ugh... We are not making detours, we are not risking any more trouble, especially not for me. Seriously Eric, I'm not that important.'

That last statement had an odd weight to it. It felt to Eric as though something about Finn's personality had clicked into place, obviously something that he didn't like to talk about, but he had just scratched the surface of what the problem was, and felt the need to press the matter.

'What do you mean, you're not that important?!' Eric asked, accusingly.

Finn sighed, feeling as though he didn't have the energy for an argument, and decided to explain himself.

'What I mean is, this whole "you getting abducted and turned into a monster" thing is putting you on my conscience, and I want it to be clear. When this is all over, I would be more than happy if we just went our separate ways and forget this ever happened.'

'So what? So you can go back to living like a hermit and feeling sorry for yourself?'

Eric drew up to Finn so that they were shoulder to shoulder.

'What happened to you when we were trying to get in the office? You weren't so miserable then,' Eric reasoned.

Finn looked away and sneered.

'I let my guard down, just this once. I don't need to tell you that I'm a horrible friend. I've said it before, so just let it be...'

It was clear that Eric wasn't getting through to him, and it was getting on his nerves, how stubborn he was behaving. Of all the people that Eric had expected to come to his aid when he was taken away, Finn was the last that he ever thought would step in to attempt a rescue, but the fact that he had, showed that there was more to him than the grumpy, self-centred loner that he often appeared to be. There was a part of him that did genuinely care about him. He had revealed that to Eric, and it was up to him to remind him of that.

'"You are my responsibility".'

Finn turned slowly and looked at Eric.

'Excuse me?' Finn asked, confused after hearing the sound of his own voice.

'That's what you said. When I got dragged down here, I didn't think I was worth saving, because I've only ever messed up in life, but you told me that you would look after me'

'Yeah? What's your point?' Finn questioned, folding his arms.

'My point is that I'm not going to let you risk your life for me, just so that you can put yourself down for the sake of it! You're not a horrible friend, so let's get some food, so you can start feeling better about yourself, okay?'

Swooping behind his friend, Eric slotted his hands under Finn's arms and lifted him off of the ground, startling the man and causing him to flail as his balance was thrown off.

'Eric! What the hell!? Put me down!'

Straining only slightly, it was apparent now that his strength had increased somewhat, as he wouldn't have been able to lift a person of Finn's size for a long period of time, but now it felt as though he could go for a couple minutes at least, and would have had little trouble with lifting him along if his passenger wasn't struggling so much. With his protests falling on deaf ears, Eric flew through the corridors with the man held out in front of him, until they had both arrived at the entrance to the mess hall, and then gently lowered Finn back onto his feet, where he turned to face the ex-human and glared at him.

'Honestly… I could have walked,' Finn grumbled, as Eric pushed the door open and ushered him in.

'Yeah? And if you collapsed, that wouldn't do either of us any good,' Eric interjected. 'I'm going to see what they've got stored in the kitchen, in the meantime, please just find a table and take it easy'

Outside of the hours that the mess hall was being staffed, the room was dead quiet, making it fairly easy for Eric to hear the sound of Finn pulling up a chair after he had turned his back to search through the contents of the next room. Vaulting over the counter, Eric crept into the kitchen, taking a cautionary sweep of his surroundings to make sure that the room was unoccupied, and found this to be the case. The kitchen itself was of a typical design, if a little rundown, and thankfully for Eric, the ovens had been left turned off for long enough that the space had returned to room temperature.

Eric rubbed his palms together and then selected the first cupboard.

Alright, what's in this one? Some bread? That'll do nicely... a couple slices of cheese... I wonder if they're keeping any meat around here?

From his seat in the abandoned mess hall, Finn could faintly hear the sounds of his partner, rummaging around in the kitchen. Doors opening and closing, pots and pans knocking together, and after a while, a painful yelp. Finn rushed over to the counter upon hearing it, and found Eric, running one of his hands under a tap with his eyes screwed shut, chittering quietly to himself.

'Are you alright in there, Eric? What happened?' Finn called out to him.

The boy snapped himself out of his trance, and with his free hand, waved back at the man.

'I'm okay! I just touched a hot pipe at the back of one of the cupboards,' he replied.

Finn took a glance towards the sink and inspected it from a distance. Blood was oozing out of Eric's palm and mixing with the water as it splashed over his wound, which had tuned black and was beginning to come away in small chunks.

'Jeez... You be bloody careful from now on. I may not know much about the people living down here, but what I do know is that anything hot is bad news for them,' he warned.

Eric, having sufficiently cooled down his injury, turned off the tap and withdrew his hand from the sink.

'Thanks Finn, I'll remember that... You can go back now. I've almost got everything ready'

Watching him leave the counter, Eric caught a concerned look from Finn as he left for his table. His reaction was quite dire, and after getting a good look at the hand that he had been running under the tap, he understood why. The flesh around where he had touched the pipe had gone a considerably darker tone and peeled back, revealing a sore and angry shade of pink underneath. It wasn't the worst pain that he had been through, but it was still enough to make him wince, especially when the blood that was escaping from it began to sizzle, now that it wasn't being immediately washed off of him. Eric mused that the sensation was a lot like holding a fistful of popping candy, and drew his nose close to it, letting his curiosity get the better of him, then recoiled in disgust when the stench of it hit him, causing the boy to gag.

Having recovered, Eric set about retrieving the last of the ingredients that he was searching for, and after a short while, exited the kitchen with two plates in hand. Finn saw him coming with the food and drained some water into a pair of cups from a water cooler set at the end of the table, and took a sip as Eric's creation was set down in front of him. After being convinced that their safety was assured, Finn took out the revolver, which had been stuffed uncomfortably into one of his side-pockets, and laid it on the table.

'So… This is interesting,' he commented, lifting up the top slice of bread to inspect the layers of fillings underneath.

Eric scooped up his own sandwich, being careful of the bandaged spot on his hand, and held it up to his jaws, wondering how he would go about eating it.

'It's not a family recipe or anything,' the skulker replied, modestly. 'Just something that I threw together and hoped for the best'

After taking a look at the fillings that Eric had chosen, Finn folded the lid back on and tucked in, taking a few bites out of it, before stopping to observe Eric, who was still pondering his angle of approach. The sandwich hovered over his snout, which tilted this way and that, as he thought about the best way of getting it in without making a mess. He tried fitting it in from the side, and then took it out again, worrying that the strength of his bite would cause the contents of his sandwich to rocket out of the sides when he bit down on it, and instead had a different idea, and moved it to the space above his upper jaws.

Taking another bite of the sandwich that Eric had made for him, Finn watched curiously, as Eric opened his upper set of jaws, like the doors on a space shuttle, and parked the sandwich on the middle of his tongue, before closing them again with the sandwich inside. In a moment of pure instinct, Eric moved his meal to one side of his mouth, where the teeth there began moving of their own accord, cutting the bread, cheese, lettuce and tomato into smaller chunks and then passing them further back, where, by the time that they had reached the back of his mouth, they were small enough to swallow. When it was over, Eric breathed a sigh of relief, having discovered that eating as a skulker was a lot less hassle than he had first anticipated, and then noticed that Finn had been staring at him while it was going on.

'I'm sorry... That wasn't too weird, was it?' he asked, feeling somewhat embarrassed.

Finn shrugged.

'At the end of the day, I intend for that doctor to keep his word, so it won't be bothering you too much longer... This is some good food, though,' Finn praised, changing the subject.

'Oh, really? I'm glad you like it!' Eric beamed.

Starting to show the beginnings of a smile curling at the corners of his lips, Finn finished off the last piece and washed it down with a gulp of water.

'I think you did a great job there. I'm feeling better already.'

It was starting to dawn on Finn that what Eric had said about him was right, he was starting to feel a lot better already, having eaten something and replenished his energy. It had given Finn the right mood and the time to think about what he was going to do with his life after the current events had reached a conclusion, and that perhaps, opening up to people wasn't such a bad idea after all.

Thunk

Jarred from their relaxation, Finn and Eric were startled by the sound of something moving heavily, accompanied by the sound of scraping metal coming from above them. Keeping a close eye on the ceiling, they listened as it travelled deeper into the room, before heading towards the kitchen. Nervously, and while still fixated on the steadily fading noise, Eric picked up his paper cup and carefully tipped some of the water over his head.

Finn returned his gaze to Eric and leaned over with a dubious expression.

'I think that's our cue to get the hell out of here, don't you?' he whispered to Eric, who had emptied his cup and stood up from his seat, looking at the room on the far end of the mess hall with a worried look on his face, and then back to Finn, before taking his cue and leaving the table with Finn in tow.

'It's a bit awkward that we have to leave just yet, but I can see where you're right. We're not out of the fire yet, and I really don't like the sound of whatever that is moving around up there,' he said, following his path back to where they had entered in from, and then reaching for the door handle. It was only after pulling down on the handle that his eyes met with those belonging to another, gleaming with the same dull yellow as his own.

Both Finn and Eric backed away from the entrance, as one after another, a total of four skulkers, all unintroduced to the two of them, pushed their way into the room and began hunting around, upending some of the chairs and tables. When one of them caught sight of Finn, they grouped together and made a beeline for him, barging past Eric as they did. Finn was intimidated, but not nearly as much as how righteously angry he was made by that.

'Hey, What the hell was that for? He wasn't doing anything to you!' Finn shouted.

Stopping just short of him, the four were quick to surround him, and the apparent leader squared up to face Finn at the front. Being surrounded on all sides by them was quickly starting to feel like being trapped in a boiler room, especially with them all breathing down his neck. Finn tried to keep his composure, but the sweat beading on his forehead betrayed him nonetheless.

'We were hoping we would run into you...' he sneered. 'Finn Lacksley, the brave little human who came all the way down here to help break us out, isn't that right?'

Finn cringed, but held his eye contact.

'I just got dragged into this. What's it to you?'

'Oh? You just got dragged into this, did you?'

Finn found himself being manhandled by the group of skulkers, who roughly grabbed him by the arms and rooted through his pockets, before pulling out the metal case and taking it.

'So this is what our doctor asked you to get for him, is it?' the leader asked, snidely.

Finn panicked and tried to grab it back from them, earning himself a punch in the gut for his trouble. He could tell that the blow was restrained, but it was still easily enough to wind him, and he gasped, trying to get his breath back while the leader started off again.

'He sent you to get this for him. He could have asked anyone, but he asked you. Do you know what that means?'

Finn stayed silent, but answered when one of the leader's goons slapped him lightly on the side of his face and commanded him to speak.

'Beats me,' he coughed.

The skulkers shared a glance, causing Finn to wince, fearing that they would take his response literally. Thankfully they did not.

'What it means,' the leader explained, 'is that you're in line to become one of his favourites.'

'Only a select few of us get that privilege,' another joined in.

Finn put his hands up defensively and stared down the lead skulker.

'I can assure you, I have no interest in that. Honestly, I would like it if I never had to see him or any of "this" ever again, but I need that case, or else he isn't going to hold up his end of the bargain.'

Taking the case from another of the group, the lead skulker opened the cap and peeked inside, grinning wickedly, and then closed it and returned his attention to Finn.

'Sorry... We're grateful for all the help you've given us, being a big distraction for that muscle head who used to run this place, but we're going to be the ones delivering this. And if we were to tell our doctor that you just happened to have an "unfortunate accident" on your way back, then I'm sure he would understand,' the leader menaced, drawing a clawed hand ever closer to Finn's neck, until he stopped just short of Finn jugular, feeling something press up to the back of his head.

'You b-back off of him, right now!'

The voice belonged to Eric, and while it was clear that he was using it to assert authority, there was an anxious falter in the way he said it. He had taken the revolver that Finn had been given for his protection, off the table, and it was now pressed against the base of the lead skulker's skull.

Slowly, the skulkers surrounding Finn moved away from the battered man and focused their attention on Eric, creeping either side of him while their leader faced Eric down.

'Now, it doesn't matter to me what happens to that case, take it and leave,' Eric told them.

Finn glared from over the leader's shoulder.

'Oh yes it does!' Finn shouted. 'I've come all this way, there is no way in hell that I'm going to quit now!'

Quickly grabbing for the case, Finn got into a tussle with the lead skulker, while Eric struggled to keep the other three under control. This lasted until Eric fired a warning shot into one of the nearby tables, causing all four of them to freeze on the spot. In the ensuing silence the sound of something moving in the adjacent room caught the attention of one of the skulkers, who signalled it to their leader. The leader of the group clicked his teeth irritably and cleared some space, before weighing the case in his hand.

'Hmm... Now that gives me an idea...'

The leader of the group raised the case up so that they could all see it, and then wound back and threw it through the gap separating the mess hall from the kitchen, where it clattered onto the floor somewhere in the next room.

'If you want it so badly, why don't you come with us and get it?'

Finn hesitated and weighed his options, but in the end, he had to agree. He wasn't stupid, he'd heard what was going on before the group had entered the room, and by his guess, that sound from earlier was another one of the skulker's party entering in from a different route. They were leading him into a trap, but even if he ended up falling for it, the case was Finn's insurance that the doctor was going to keep his word. As the whole group moved through the mess hall and into the kitchen, a voice echoed from the far end, coming from beyond a heavy, metal door which had been left open, exuding a cool mist that billowed out softly onto the tiled floor of the kitchen.

'Hey, guys! I found him! Are you going to come and help, or what?'

The lead skulker smirked.

'That sounds like Charlie got a hold of our old friend Max. Let's just say he's been feeling a little poorly lately and happened to slip his leash. We were in the middle of tracking him down when we ran into you two,' he explained to Eric and Finn, before turning back towards the walk-in freezer ahead of them and replying to his unseen companion. 'I hear you in there! Don't start anything without us!'

When they got inside, the first thing of note was the serious lack of anyone else present. The freezer was expansive, big enough to house enough frozen food for the denizens of the building to last at least a couple of months, owing greatly to the layout of the building that it catered for. The building itself was built like a doomsday bunker and had a stockpile of supplies to match, frost-covered packages lined every wall from top to bottom, illuminated by an eerie fluorescent glow which emanated from light fixtures set into the ceiling. Just past the entrance lay the spot where the case had landed, having chipped part of the cap off as it hit the ice-encrusted floor. The group of six entered further into the room cautiously, wary of the dim lighting and slippery footing. It was only the one human among them that found themselves put off by the sharp drop in temperature, chattering his teeth and rubbing his arms to keep warm.

'Jeez, I thought it was cold out there. What is it? Minus twenty in here?' Finn complained.

Falling behind the other skulkers, Eric joined Finn and contemplated his surroundings.

'I guess… I should feel cold, we're in a freezer after all. It just feels… kind of nice. It's hard to describe,' Eric admitted.

Finn shivered, setting his sights on the case.

'Alright, we'll get it back and get out of here. As soon as that guy they're waiting for turns up, be prepared to run like hell,' Finn whispered closely.

Nearby where the case had fallen was a curtain made of flat plastic strips, made to separate one section of the freezer from another, behind them something rustled.

'Hey Charlie! Did you get lost? What are you doing in there?' the leader called.

No response.

'You found him, so where is he? Don't tell me that you had all the fun to yourself and left nothing for us. That's not how this is supposed to…'

There was blood on the curtains. It might have been from some frozen meat, but then surely the workers who stocked the freezer would have been more careful with it, and not dragged it along the floor, leaving a trail that exited from behind the curtains and wound around a corner, to a space behind this closed area.

'Something's not right,' the leader warned, and stepped around the curtained room slowly, following the trail until he had encountered its source. A section of the freezer's ventilation had dropped from where it was pinned to the ceiling some time ago, and now lay on the floor, split open from the inside. Whatever was inside it had burst out, like an insect emerging from a cocoon, leaving behind a shell of metal, and something bloody and mangled resting within.

'So... This is what happened to old Max, is it? I knew he wouldn't survive! He was unworthy to even dream he could be one of us!' The lead skulker laughed triumphantly.

As the four skulkers gathered around to inspect their discovery, Finn took the time to take advantage of this distraction and pocket the case. He and Eric now had a window of opportunity, one that they would be taking advantage of shortly, had they not been distracted by the change in the group's mood when one of the four picked something out of the mangled mess and held it up into the light.

'Hey, boss... This is... It's Charlie...' the skulker whimpered.

'What!? How!? You're lying! Give it to me!' the leader snarled, snatching the slimy object from his fellow's hands.

He stared deeply at it, and it stared back, except the stare that it returned was vacant and unblinking. The leader of the skulkers was growing more horrified by the second, and it showed in his companions. Dropping what he was holding, the skull of his former companion fell into the pile of entrails which it had been fished out of with a morbid squelch, and the leader turned to address the rest of his team. There was fear in his eyes, but it turned into a burning hatred as he made his speech.

'I'm not going to let this happen again. When we next find Max, we're going to attack him all at once. Now, who was keeping an eye on those two losers?'

The leader glared at Finn and Eric, who had started to escape from the freezer, and yelled after them.

'They're getting away, you idiots! Don't let them escape!'

Running at full speed to give chase to them, the skulkers barely noticed when one of their number suddenly felt a sharp pain in his legs and found himself being pulled backwards at an incredible speed, under the plastic dividers that the group had seen when they first entered the freezer, and into a new room, where large chunks of meat hung on hooks, some with large and irregular bites taken out of them, and the stench of something foul and thick filling the air. This skulker desperately tried to scrabble to get himself upright, scraping his claws on the tiled floor and only succeeding so much as to turn himself onto his back to get a sight at what was pulling him, a sight that gave him no doubts as to how his former companion had been found in such a gruesome state, and the fate would soon be befalling him.

A whole section of heavy kitchen utensils was pulled off a wall in the mess hall's kitchen, and were thrown backwards, where they collided with the bodies of several chasing skulkers, causing them to stumble when the first one tripped, sending the others behind him tumbling over the one in the lead. Eric and Finn had got what they came for and were making their escape, and while Eric was still in possession of the firearm that had been passed between the two of them, he was reluctant to use it on a living being, and so, wouldn't use it if he didn't need to. Having been successful in slowing down their pursuers, Eric helped Finn to climb over the counter and into the mess hall, before clambering over the top of it himself, and while he did so, the skulkers behind them had been fast to recover and were closing the distance.

Neither of them knew if they could outrun the group who were chasing after them, but regardless, they were making a break for the doors, so that they could leave the mess hall and be heading in the direction of the exit, trying to put as much distance between them as possible. When they had made it past the rows of tables and chairs, Finn glanced back, to see that the skulkers were in the midst of vaulting over the counter themselves, when a scream came blasting out of the kitchen, and as the two pursuers turned in the direction of where it had come from, a third skulker who had been lagging behind the pair, bulldozed his way into them, knocking them over the other side. Having been shoved over the counter and onto the floor, the leader of the group began to pick himself up and protest, before backing away frantically.

A huge foreboding shape loomed over the back of the skulker who was still trapped behind the counter, who felt himself being pinned down by something heavy and reeking of blood. From this shape emerged jaws that, while of a similar shape to those of his own, were much larger, big enough that all light in the room was blotted out when they closed around his head. The pinned skulker screamed and thrashed, but it was no use, the creature that had a hold of him was far stronger, and his struggles only served to drive it into a frenzy. Soon the creature was shaking the skulker's body like a terrier with a rat, throwing it from side to side with such ferocity that an audible snap of bone could be heard each time that it was pulled the other way. Not even a minute into the violent mauling and the limp body flew loose of the creature's maw, headless, and crashed into a row of tables nearby.

Leaping up onto the counter, the creature revealed itself to be a large and horrifying mutant skulker, taking a form very familiar of the beast-skulkers that Finn had seen, caged within another area of the building some time ago, only this one was much more imposing. It stood on all-fours, covered in muscle and painted red, the only vestiges of who it once was being the few scraps of camouflage patterned fabric that clung to it loosely. It finally opened its jaws again, releasing a torrent of blood and a hard lump of pulp that used to be another skulker's head onto the floor, and began a guttural panting, expelling puffs of steam from its dripping jaws. While the leader of the group of skulkers scrambled to hide under something, the beast jumped down from the counter and on top of the other skulker who had been shoved onto the floor, breaking the helpless skulker's neck with its sheer weight. Then, its eyes became transfixed on the only human in the room, who stared back at it from the other end of the mess hall, frozen in abject terror. The creature's whole body started to jitter, as if it was suddenly boiling with rage, and it rattled its teeth, staring dead at him.

'...crcrcrcCRCRCRCRRRR... LACCCKSLEEY!!!' The beast roared in his direction.

Finn's heart stopped. Even after transforming into an abomination, far more terrifying than his wildest nightmares, it had remembered him, and he was now the target of its murderous rage. Finn squeaked, his scream catching in his dry throat.

'Oh, eff this!' he yelled, grabbing Eric by the arm and dashing out into the hallway.

In response to seeing its prey take flight, the mutant skulker formerly known as Maxwell let lose a blood-curdling screech and launched itself forwards, beginning the hunt.

CHAPTER SEVENTEEN

D eep inside the underground facility, and far too far away from any way out, the hallway that Finn Lacksley and Eric Jones had entered once again filled with the echoes of their racing footfalls, both of them running as fast as their legs would carry them, as further back, the doors to the mess hall that they had so urgently left behind tore off of their hinges, as the monstrous body of the mutated Maxwell ploughed through them. The hulking beast locked on to the escaping duo and released another deafening cry, before splitting its over-sized jaws into a Y-shaped flower of death, and charged, ripping deep claw marks into the ground as it barreled after them.

The thunderous sound of the monster behind him was beginning to make Finn sweat. It was getting closer far too quickly, and the only thing he could do was keep running, in the hope that somewhere down the line he could either outrun it or find a place to hide, however, in an instant, those hopes were dashed. The monster had caught up with them far quicker than either of them were able to outpace, and the first to feel the immediate consequence of that was Finn, who yelped as the creature's fore-claws slashed horizontally across the back of his right calf.

Eric spun upon watching Finn drop from his side and skid onto his front. His mentor's whole back was exposed to the monster, and if he didn't do something, he would be ripped to shreds in no time at all. The former human mercenary, turned abomination, stalked over to where Finn had fallen, completely oblivious of his partner, and stepped on his back to stop him from escaping, inching his horrifyingly large maw ever closer. From Eric's perspective, this was far too much to bear. He still had the gun, which he pointed at the monster leaning over Finn's prone body, but his hands were trembling. He had fired a warning shot before, but during that time, he was intentionally trying to miss, now there was no certainty that he wouldn't have to use it on something living.

'Don't make me do this...'

Grimacing, Finn looked up at Eric from under it and spoke to him softly so as not to signal his fear to the monster of his back.

'Bloody hell, Eric. Just shoot the bloody thing already...'

Eric's hands couldn't stop shaking, he wanted to shoot it, but his fingers wouldn't depress the trigger, and his eyelids scrunched up with fear. Maxwell was close now. He could smell the fear from his human prey, and with great satisfaction, bent his jaws so that they draped over the tops of Finn's shoulders, sending the lower jaw to run down his spine, and slowly began to squeeze. The new, animal part of his brain was telling him to kill and consume him right away, but for now, the part of him that was still human had more control, and it was this part of him that wanted Finn to suffer. The mutant's bloodshot eyes widened madly as his teeth clamped down, puncturing the padding on Finn's overalls, sinking past it and piercing the man's skin, causing him to yell, but before he could get very far, there was another pain, this time – his own. The creature released Finn quickly upon something sharp tearing into its back, snapping around to see the last remaining skulker of the group that it had hunted down, meeting its gaze with his claws primed and jaws unlocked.

'You killed all of them... All of my friends! Maxwell! I will make you BLEED!' the skulker bellowed at the monster, before launching into another attack.

Taking advantage of the distraction, Eric moved to where Finn lay, pulling him to his feet and checking to make sure that he wasn't too badly hurt. While assisting Finn to run, the skulkers behind them snapped and clawed at each other furiously, until Maxwell had once again gained the upper hand and overpowered the former leader, smashing him to the ground viciously.

Upon hearing the screams and sounds of tearing flesh behind them, Finn looked to Eric, who was holding him by the shoulder.

'Don't look back, keep moving,' he counselled. 'Unless we want to end up like them, then we have to get out of here.'

Making use of the time that the both of them had been afforded, the duo entered into a stairwell leading to the ground floor. Without anything to barricade the door with, the creature chasing them was going to come crashing through sooner rather than later, and so, the two of them descended with haste. It was just as they reached the bottom that above them, another crash could be heard and chunks of door rained down over their heads.

Bolting into the first room they could find, Eric slammed the door shut and braced it as hard as he could while Finn searched for something to block it off. There was a large metal cabinet close by, which he strained to upend in front of the entrance, but even with that much weight, it wouldn't be enough. Turning around to get a better idea of where they were, he and Eric were met by the sight of a large truck being suspended on a pair of metal struts; the last one left within a garage which seemed to have been recently vacated. Nearby, there was an airlock. Finn didn't immediately recognise it, but in the back of his mind, he knew that this was the other side of the bulkhead that Eric had first been taken in by.

In his haste to find something stronger to hold the doors shut, Finn had neglected to help fortify the barricade that they had erected, and an impact on the other side had caused the contents of the shelf to skid across the floor, including a collection of bright red tubes that fell by Eric's feet. An eerie call emanated from behind the makeshift blockade. Again, the creature called Finn's name. Finn was overwhelmed with fear, but swallowed it down and approached Eric solemnly.

'Okay mate, I hate to say this, but I'm going to need that gun. I'll do you a swap,' he said, exchanging the doctor's case with the revolver.

Eric wasn't eager to let go, and stared at him questioningly.

'What's the plan now, Finn? Are we going to try and take him on? Even with the gun, I don't know if that's going to work…'

There was a tense moment between them. Eric could tell by Finn's expression that what he was about to say next wasn't something that he wanted to hear.

'Eric… You're a smart lad, you've got your whole life ahead of you.'

Eric's eyes were beginning to well up.

'This thing that's chasing us – chasing me, rather – it's only after me. If we both go out of those doors, it'll break through and kill the both of us.'

'No, you can't be serious!' Eric cried.

Finn pushed out the chamber and inspected how many bullets were left, staring into the empty slots dejectedly, before pushing it back into place.

'In a minute, you're going to stop holding him back and you're going to get out through this exit as fast as you can. Keep going until you're at the elevator at the end of the cave, and when you reach the surface, take that case to the doctor and get yourself fixed.'

Eric's grip was failing and the battering from behind him was only getting stronger, but he was reluctant to go, and shook his head, denying that he would leave Finn to slow down the monster while he escaped.

'But... but... maybe if we work together, as a team, we could still beat him. There's got to be something we can do.'

Finn pulled a lever next to the bulkhead, causing the emergency release to kick in, and gradually the doors slid open. After a brief look outside into the dank air of the cavern, he lifted the collar of his uniform to inspect where he had been bitten. The wounds weren't deep, but they had covered a large portion of his body and stung when he moved a certain way. They would cause a problem if he had to manoeuvre quickly. Taking this into account, he didn't fancy his chances, but at this point they no longer concerned him. Showing Eric the door, he signalled for him to go.

'No. I'm not leaving! I'm not letting you sacrifice yourself—'

Finn glared.

'I'm only going to bother telling you this once, before I get really mad with you, Eric! Stop being a brat and get out of here!' Finn shouted.

Eric shivered. In that moment, Finn had decided his fate. Respecting his wishes and leaving felt too much like the wrong thing to do. He felt a cramp in his gut when he thought about leaving him behind, especially after what they had been through, and knowing what was likely to happen to him afterwards, but Finn had made it clear that there was no other choice, and with a heavy heart, Eric disengaged himself from the barricade.

With the case securely tucked away, Eric flew past and out into the moist air beyond the bulkhead, and not a moment too soon, as the creature that he had been preventing from getting into the garage, the former mercenary leader turned abominable skulker, burst through the barricade, sending the metal shelving scraping across the floor with his monstrous force. It was evident from the foaming scars, that the beast had not come away unscathed from its scrap with the skulker upstairs, but if it had truly been hampered in any way, it wasn't showing it. Backing away slowly in order to cover himself more effectively behind the truck, Finn levelled his weapon and waited for it to make the first move.

There was every chance within the next few seconds that the creature would launch into a frenzy, but for now, it was sizing him up, pacing around the side of the truck like a lion toying with its food. Finn had to admit, he was more scared for his own life now than ever before, but he had succeeded in drawing the attention away from Eric, allowing him to escape, and that was what he had come here to do. If he was going to die soon, then he would be doing it with his conscience cleared.

'So, what are you bloody waiting for? Are you gonna kill me, or what?! You piece of trash!'

Soon after his challenge, the creature leaned its head over the front bonnet of the truck, showing off its rows of hooked fangs and a maddened, twitching gaze. Reaching a gargantuan claw over, it scratched into the metal, cleaving off the paintwork and summoning forth a sound that assaulted Finn's eardrums. When it was done, the beast clicked furiously, signalling its anger towards him, before reaching up, looking to climb over the obstacle separating them and further drive him into a corner. Not looking to leave by the same route that Eric had taken, Finn had to think fast, as the skulker's next move would be to pounce down and tear him limb from limb, and so, he would go underneath, moving to hide from the mutant skulker once again.

Under the truck, Finn could hear the ominous click of the monster above him. It was getting seriously frustrated now, digging at the roof of the vehicle above him, which turned to pounding as Finn refused to be scared out from under it. He could feel the truck rocking, but despite his fear, he wasn't going to let this animal psyche him out. He had formulated a plan, a risky and likely ineffective plan, but a plan nonetheless. All he had to do was wait for it to snap. Finally, the skulker got impatient and leapt down to the floor, just as Finn had expected, and as it dived under the truck trying to catch him in its jaws and pull him out, Finn rolled out the other way, narrowly avoiding its oversized maw, and ended up on the other side of the truck.

Being roughly the size of a grizzly bear, it was a tight squeeze for the monstrosity to get its whole body underneath the truck, but Finn's tricks had made it furious, and this was the second time that he had managed to escape from its clutches, he wasn't going to get away a third time. It crawled in after him, and only after getting halfway through, did the feral skulker realize that it was being lured into a trap. But before it could pull itself out, the platform that had been suspending the truck above it began to lower, trapping the beast in place.

Finn breathed a sigh of relief, panting as his heart rate lowered, and with his thumb still pressing down on the control switch. He had turned the tables on the former mercenary leader, and watched as it howled and struggled under the weight bearing down on it. Dismayingly, the mechanism got stuck soon after it had pinned the beast down, and trying to force it any further only resulted in the gears making a horrible crunching sound as they ground against one another, but at this point the machine had done more than enough. He now had a clear shot at the monster's head.

Even though it had tried, and nearly succeeded in killing him, both before and after its transformation, it wasn't without some pity that Finn had decided on shooting the trapped creature. Strings of blood and saliva hung from its snarling visage, it's bloodshot eyes boring into Finn, as if willing him to burst into flames. This was the face of a creature that had lost the precious things that made it human, succumbing to a fate that Finn wouldn't wish on anyone. Momentarily, his thoughts drifted back to the room filled with cages, wondering how many others had shared his fate, although it was not something that he would dwell on for long, as he had to finish what he had started.

Aiming the mercenary leader's firearm at a point between the eyes of its former owner, Finn discharged the weapon, causing a crack to reverberate around the garage's empty space. The impact area of the bullet had been slightly above where Finn had intended it to hit as a result of the weapon's tremendous recoil, and it had smacked into the top creature's skull, tearing off the soft tissue on its forehead and exposing the hard bone beneath. While the bullet hadn't managed to penetrate the thick skull of the skulker, Finn was sure that the creature was dead, or at the very least brain-damaged. It had ceased moving, and lay with its neck slack and head tilted to the side, clawed fingers twitching reflexively.

Killing the monster that Maxwell had become, hadn't given Finn any sense of joy or relief that something which had put his life in danger would no longer be troubling him; the action had purely been taken for the assurance that his own survival wouldn't be put in jeopardy. Having to take a moment to reflect, Finn let the revolver fall to the ground. Seeing as the last round of ammunition had been spent, he had no more use for it. Having essentially murdered someone was a difficult concept to digest, but there were too many events that were simply out of Finn's control, and there were still many questions left unanswered, and with a nagging feeling that the worst was still yet to come, Finn turned to leave the building by its main exit.

...crcrcr...

The sound began softly. Finn had almost missed it. He had to check again to confirm that his suspicions were correct, and cursed as the clicking grew in intensity, soon joined by the sound of straining metal. Alive, and blind with rage, the mutant skulker that Finn had thought dead had survived, and was now using all of its strength to wrench the platform from on top of it, pushing up with such a savage power that the whole platform was starting to tear off of its support struts. Finn tried to make a run for the exit, but in a sudden turn of events, the platform, with the truck resting on top of it snapped lose, and he felt a rush of air as it was hurled towards him.

Survival reflexes kicking in, Finn had to dive backwards or end up getting crushed under the weight of the vehicle which had been thrown his way, landing on his back and tearing at the bite wounds that tracked along either side of his spine. He was in definite pain now, and could feel the clothes he was wearing getting damp with his blood, but this would pale in comparison to the pain that he would be feeling very shortly. Pulling itself up onto its feet, the skulker once again had full view of the human that it had been hunting, now wounded and vulnerable. It was the perfect time to strike.

Lying on his back, Finn watched as the skulker split its jaws apart, preparing to charge, and not wanting to face the creature when it put an end to his life, he turned his eyes away from it, looking instead to the exit and lamenting how close he had come to it after all that he had been through. Just as he was watching it, something that he couldn't explain began to take place, something that he was sure was an illusion cast by the throes of being so close to his own demise. Out of the darkness of the cave beyond the door, came a brilliant red light, which grew brighter and brighter, until it had finally entered into the room, where it shone like a fallen star, casting the forms of both Finn and the behemoth in it's overwhelming radiance. Finn had to shield his eyes from the intensity of the sudden light, but through his fingers, he could just about make out the outline of someone that he hadn't expected to come back for him. It was Eric, standing defiantly, his fist a burning ball of energy, and with an expression more confident than he had ever seen him with before.

'Eric, what the hell are you doing?'

Eric readied himself.

'I said that I wasn't going to let you sacrifice yourself. I'm going to get you out of here, if it's the last thing I do!'

Having been enraged by yet another interruption, the abominable skulker switched targets and galloped towards

Eric, who met its charge head on, and in an act that baffled Finn, he rammed his fist into the beast's mouth, driving the blazing ball of energy down it's throat, where it glowed brightly under the surface of its near translucent hide. Such a maneuver was not without consequences however, and Eric Jones discovered quite quickly, that the consequences he would be suffering were going to hurt. A lot.

Immediately, Eric's hand, his wrist, all the way up to his forearm, was engulfed by the extreme pressure of the jaws closing down on him. Screaming, Eric tried to punch and claw at the jaws locked around his arm, but it was only getting worse as he struggled. Hundreds of razor-sharp teeth stabbed deep into his flesh, and the strength of the creature's bite was causing his bones to crack. Soon enough, both Finn and Eric heard the sickening snap of the boy's arm separating into two pieces, blood pouring from the sides of the feral skulker's mouth as it continued to crunch through his limb.

'Have you lost your mind!? He's going to take your arm off!' Finn yelled, as Eric desperately tried to yank his arm out of the creature's mouth.

'I… I know what I'm doing,' he replied through the pain.

With a great amount of effort, Eric managed to rip himself free, but not without losing the portion of his arm that the larger skulker had taken. His forearm now ended in a torn and gushing stump, sporting the gruesome sight of his splintered bones poking out of the ripped end. The excruciating experience of having his wrist broken and torn off had brought Eric to his knees, cradling the ruined arm and weeping. Finn could barely bring himself to watch.

'Eric! Come on, get up!' Finn cried. 'I tried fighting and it didn't work! You have to get away before he…'

The creature moved backwards suddenly, eyes bulging and breath quickening. Something had changed in the beast after it had swallowed Eric's arm. Its stomach was heaving and it looked like it was going to be sick. Staggering, the creature gurgled as blood and smoke began to fountain out of its maw, it's underbelly starting to turn an unpleasant colour.

'Those things over there... It took me a while... But I found out what they were...' Eric mumbled, pointing Finn's gaze towards a handful red tubes that lay scattered close to where they had entered from. '...They're flares...'

Shuddering from the agonizing presence of the burning object inside of it, the skulker's attempts to regurgitate the flare became desperate, as inside of it, the creature's organs were being liquefied by the intense heat. As Finn dragged himself away, fearing that it would make a last-ditch effort to lash out at the both of them, the creature released one last choking screech before its stomach ruptured, spilling out a tidal wave of melted innards onto the garage floor, where they simmered under the shaking creature. The sight alone was enough to make the bile rise in Finn's throat, but that smell was truly revolting, even Eric was struggling to cope with the nauseating fumes that the skulker's ruined abdomen was emitting. Most of the muscle that had been supporting the skulker's middle had been damaged, and continued to degrade until there was no longer enough to support the beast's weight, and it collapsed, with the corroded spinal column breaking apart and severing the connection between its torso and its pelvis. Having in mere moments been utterly destroyed by the flare, the abomination rattled its teeth pitifully, slowly losing the power to claw one half of its body towards the pair, before it finally fell down and stopped moving.

Getting up tentatively so as to not hurt himself further, Finn staggered over to his companion and gripped him by the shoulders. The wound to Eric's arm had foamed over, but there was still far too much leaking through, and so Finn hurriedly unfastened the top of his bloodied worker's overalls, and got Eric to bite into it, tearing it into strips which he made into a makeshift bandage.

'I-it hurts! It really hurts! Oh God, that was so stupid of me!'

Finn fastened the bandage and knelt down, getting Eric's attention.

'Eric, honestly. I want you to focus. We're getting out of here, right now. The both of us. Grab a hold of my arm and keep with me,' Finn instructed, guiding the boy to take a hold of him.

Arms over each other's shoulders for support, Finn and Eric left behind the carcass of the mutant skulker, walking past the overturned military truck and out of the doorway which led to the cavern outside. Here was the path of planks and stone that stretched all the way from the building and the shimmering lake, to the far wall, where the elevator to the outside world resided. Along the haphazard path, distant voices could be heard, echoing through the empty space, getting closer as the pair drew nearer. Lurking amongst the shadows, in damp areas of the cave, were other skulkers, some simply milling about, and others scouting along the path away from the facility that had once been their prison, and upon catching sight of the struggling duo, a number of them converged on the pair, chattering to each other as they took them by the arms and began guiding them towards the far wall. Towards the surface.

CHAPTER EIGHTEEN

After watching the enormous cavern shutter itself from view behind the sliding doors, Finn found himself struggling to stay awake during the awkwardly cramped elevator ride. He was convinced that he needed to keep an eye on the other occupants who were taking the elevator with him and Eric, in case they did anything that he would see as suspicious. During their journey upwards, the other people taking the lift with them seemed to be enthusiastic about sharing the news of their exodus from the underground facility, providing a summary of the escape that had taken place, and more recently, the battle that had been fought on their way out. In the tone of explaining it as if it was a story of great conquest, the other skulkers told of how the divided members of Maxwell's hired guns were caught off-guard, and that even with the superior firepower at their disposal, the horde of Andrew's patients had the biological advantage, and numbers enough to overwhelm them within a matter of hours.

On arriving at the secret passageway under the basement of the factory where Finn had been working for over three years, Finn discovered that true to the story, the fight that had taken place was just as one-sided as the jubilant skulkers had made it out to be. Being hauled between pairs were the bodies of human beings, mercenaries who had fallen to the onslaught of the emerging skulkers, many of them bearing grisly lacerations, who were being carried past elevator shaft and down the stairwell, assumingly to be disposed of somewhere deeper. He and Eric tried not to focus on the skulkers moving the corpses and allowed the group to direct them out of the gloom of the underground and into the main floor of the building.

The state of Finn's former occupation was a bizarre sight to him. Never had Finn thought that he would walk through the factory that he had been working in for so long, with so much warfare having taken place. Long familiar sights had been plastered with bullet holes, scorch marks and the skulker's trademark foam… And a lot of human blood. Finn had to question whether the skulkers had been made to spare any of the men resisting their escape, but was disheartened to hear that of the opposition, very few had chosen to surrender. Feeling that the nostalgia of his workplace had been tainted by the forces that he had encountered in the world down below, Finn, with Eric at his side, was chauffeured out of the building, catching the last rays of evening sunlight filtering through the leaves of the forest nearby, as he left through the old staff entrance.

While the factory itself was only really being occupied by those left to clean up after the casualties, the large majority of the facility's residents had formed an encampment just outside the grounds, which the two were led into to be sat down and treated within one of the tents that they had pitched up within the woodland. During his time under the care of the doctor's medically inclined patients, Finn was ill at ease. Skulkers roaming about on the surface didn't sit well with him, and even if they weren't being hostile to them now, Finn didn't entirely trust them after what had gone on prior to their departure. He especially didn't trust the doctor who had made them into what they were, having kept his agendas a secret had nearly cost Finn and Eric both of their lives, and as for his future plans now that he was free, they were still a mystery. It took roughly three hours for the both of them to be patched up and allowed out of the tent; a time made more arduous by Finn's reluctance to take anaesthetics while he was having his stitches put in, paranoid that they would inject him with some of their serum. Aching and tired from his ordeals, Finn discussed with Eric his plans to speak with the doctor, opting to confront him alone.

'Are you sure that you don't want me to come along?' Eric queried, hoping that he would be of use during their conversation.

Finn looked over Eric's arm, which had been replaced with fresh bandages and a sling.

'No. The deal was between me and him, so I should be the one to hand over what's in that case of his.'

Eric looked sheepish, anxiously tugging on his sling to adjust it into a more comfortable position, before he replied.

'I get you… But he's going to bring up my future at some point. How long it'll take for me to turn back into a human, whether I'll have my arm back by that point… I'd still like to get a say. Maybe I could arrange to stay with Garth and Theo until I'm better.'

'Still, I think that it will be better if we talk alone. There are questions I have for him that might make it break down into an argument if things don't go the right way, and you don't need to be involved in that if it can't be avoided. Just take things easy for a bit, I'll be back out before you know it.'

Having been handed back the case from Eric, Finn shuffled through the swarms of skulkers prowling about the encampment, following a trail of electric torches propped along the path, towards a circular clearing, where a small community of temporary shelters had been erected. Upon his arrival to the circle, a pair of guards hailed him, and allowed him to pass into one of the nylon structures, painted on the outside with a simple "V".

Lanterns hanging from a line between the support beams of the doctor's tent illuminated a host of figures, both human and otherwise, in their orange glow. Caught in their flicker, was a character that Finn swore he recognised, speaking with the man who could positively be identified as doctor Andrew Voe, still as scraggly as before, but noticeably having made an attempt to comb his mop of hair into something more decent. As Finn approached, the curious creature perched atop the doctor's shoulder stirred, and fixed its beady eyes in his direction.

Jeez, that thing is unnerving.

It seemed as though Finn had caught the tail end of their conversation however, as the doctor pushed something into the hands of the other human and sent him on his way.

'...And be ready for that phone call, Josh. We're out of his shadow now, all that's left is to redeem that peace of mind you've earned,' the doctor called, as he left.

'Thank you, Andrew.'

Hurrying out of the doorway, Finn's eyes briefly met with the man, who for a moment was aghast with guilt, but quickly moved on before he could be stopped, disappearing out of the tent. Soon after the man's departure, the doctor took notice of his new guest and beckoned him over. The doctor's table held a number of objects, ranging from files and small devices, to a small cot, which the animal perching on his shoulder scurried off to, as Finn pulled up a seat.

'I would like to begin with my most humble apologies. I had let my grief with Maxwell get the better of me and this led to a situation where—'

'We nearly died!' Finn boomed.

Disturbed from its rest, the doctor's pet raised its head out of its cot and clicked at Finn, until Andrew offered his hand out to the small animal, letting it nuzzle against him until it returned to sleep. Starting over, the doctor began with a sigh.

'I… I recognise that what I did was a mistake. It was malicious and unnecessary, and I can't apologise enough.'

Finn unveiled the metal case that he had taken from the mercenary leader's office and placed it on the table, keeping a hand over it so that it couldn't be easily snatched away, and glared at the doctor.

'Sorry or not, I got what you wanted. What matters is that you hold up your end.'

The doctor seemed tense, cautiously inspecting the case from what he could see of it between Finn's fingers, before straightening and speaking in a more confident tone.

'From what my sources have told me, Eric had already made friends within our community, and I have little reason to doubt that he will have any trouble fitting in over the coming weeks. Should anyone be found picking on him, they will have to answer to me.'

Weeks!? It didn't take him a day to go from perfectly normal, to looking like some kind of deep-sea horror! How the hell was he going to explain to his parents that he was just gone for weeks!? That would raise all kinds of flags!'

Finn breathed through his mouth, trying to calm himself down. It was unfortunate that Eric would have to wait for so long, but at least he would be able to return to his old life, which was more than Finn could say for himself, remembering that his house had been trashed by those masked assailants, and had probably been burgled multiple times by now, Finn would have to move out, and maybe even leave the country to avoid being connected to what happened with the Silverfish warehouse. Swallowing his fears, Finn pushed the case to the other end of the table, sat up, and turned his back.

'Just so long as he gets cured. At the end of the day, I don't care what else happens. I'm off,' Finn stated summarily, making his move to leave the doctor's tent.

'Mr Lacksley... I didn't say I would cure him...'

Finn stopped dead in his tracks.

'Do you want to repeat that, doc? Because I will come over there and punch your lights out, I swear I will'

Doctor Andrew Voe ascended from his seat, standing in such a way that the light from the lanterns above him cast a shadow that eclipsed Finn completely.

'When I said that he would be normal after we reached the surface, I have made good on that promise. What you fail to realize is that people like you and me are the abnormal ones.'

Finn turned slowly, meeting the doctor again, with fire in his eyes.

'So I went and got that case for you for nothing, did I?'

The doctor huffed and popped off the cap of the metal case, pulling out the object within.

'No. I sent you to get this for me because I wanted to prove that I trusted you with a task that was crucial to my plan, and at the same time, to make it so that you wouldn't be roped into the unavoidable violence that came as a result of our break-out. Owing to my own misjudgements, that second part hadn't worked out the way I intended...'

Finn's heart rate rose. What the doctor had in his hand was a detonator, primed and ready to activate.

'… But you have my commendations for completing this task. Thanks to you, I no longer exist.'

click

There was a distant rumble. The doctor had triggered something that caused the very earth to shake beneath Finn's feet, and when Finn pulled back the fabric doorway, the doctor's meaning became frighteningly clear. A huge cloud of dust had been kicked into the air, coming from the direction of the warehouse, which grew until it loomed over the forest. A great brown monolith, rising into the black of the early night sky, with the very top of it grasping at the last vestiges of pink sunlight that had slipped below the horizon. Finn stared at the cloud rising from the rubble of his former occupation, unable to comprehend the magnitude of what he had done.

'This moment will be marked as the genesis of skulker-kind, an event that could never have happened without you. I will make it so that all of our community knows your name.'

Finn whipped around, looking quite stunned by the doctor's words and actions.

'Why the hell would I want that!? What is wrong with you!?'

'Think of this as a second chance for humanity. Maxwell was only ever interested in the spoils of war, but I have a vision of a utopia for skulkers, a truly perfect world, devoid of the ills that human society has wrought, that can only be brought about by wiping the slate clean. Every last human will be a skulker someday. I have the means, and I have made a commitment to them, my skulkers, to make that dream a reality.'

Finn shivered.

'Well, you're bloody not making me into one of those things. Not after everything I've been through, no way.'

For a moment, the doctor looked down at his desk, placing the now-inert detonator down with a melancholy expression.

'I thought that you would say that, and I must admit, I am sympathetic of what you have suffered, so I'm not going force you to join us join us just yet... You have earned a reprieve. Just know that there will be those of us out there, waiting to accept you into our ranks, and I will be waiting with them. Take care, Finn Lacksley.'

Eric stood at the foot of the road, just next to the bus shelter where he had taken his rides to and from work, practically every day for the last month. He stared out to the other side, where all that was left of warehouse 12, was a giant sinkhole, which had swallowed the building completely, along with everything within the factory's grounds and a fair amount of land outside of it. Having seen the event take place, Eric was worried about what Finn would think, and was even more worried when he actually turned up, with a mortified look on his face even before he had observed the ruins of the establishment that they had both worked at.

'We're leaving,' he said soullessly, heading towards where he had hidden his car.

Eric had to double-take to be sure Finn wasn't pulling his leg and followed behind him.

'Wha... But... What did he say? Did he say he could fix me? How long do I need to wai—'

'Just get in the damn car.'

Finn hadn't shouted, but he had ordered him in such a way as to make Eric feel like he was treading on thin ice, and so he did as he was instructed, entering into the back seat as Finn sat behind the steering wheel. With the end of his scaly snout craning over the back of the driver's seat, Eric asked him again, and that was when Finn hit the dashboard, punching it hard enough that the clear-plastic guard cracked.

'He said he won't do it, because he wants to turn everyone on earth into a skulker. I let him play me for a fool, gave him exactly what he wanted so that the police can never find him, and all because I gave him the benefit of the doubt. I knew he was crazy, and I let him win!'

Eric sunk, feeling like his whole world had collapsed in on him. It had certainly been that way for Finn also.

'So... What do I do now?' Eric asked.

Finn started the ignition and began reversing.

'We're going to my place. Nowhere else to go.'

The road had been closed all the way up to the next junction, but Finn's car easily mounted the curb and swerved around the warning signs that had been put in place, and he, with Eric in the back seat, trundled out of the scene. Behind them, if either of them had been looking, they might have seen three pale silhouettes in the blurry reflection of Finn's rear-view mirror, who watched them drive off, before slinking away into the forest.

CHAPTER NINETEEN

Finn's eyelids fluttered open. He had been sleeping, bundled up in his duvet, on his mattress on the floor, in his apartment, safe and sound. Unwrapping himself from his covers, he sat up with a yawn and stretched his arms. He had heard the sound of running water during the night, which seeing as the makeshift bed lying a short distance away from his own was empty, he would be investigating after breakfast.

Early mornings were always a pain. What hadn't always been a pain however, was the stinging sensation he got when he traced over the scars on his bare chest, tracking all the way over his shoulders and down his back, making his night's rest fraught with discomfort. Flicking the switch to get the kettle boiling, Finn picked out a mug from the tree on his counter, one with a faded Union Jack printed on it and dropped in a heaped teaspoon of coffee granules.

Another day... What's my life coming to?

While he waited for the water to be ready, Finn lazily sauntered over to the bathroom and pulled the door open a crack. The bathroom itself wasn't particularly spacious, it had just about enough room for the bath, a toilet and a sink, but you couldn't move much in there without bumping into one of them. From the little light that flowed into the room through the gap that Finn had created, he spied a pair of ivory-coloured feet, capped with a platoon of hooked talons, peeking out of a collection of soaked bath-towels that were currently piled into the bath itself. Mystery solved.

Closing the bathroom door quietly, Finn resumed the process of preparing his breakfast before he picked up his steaming mug by the handle, took it over to the windowsill by his pool table and then opened the blinds. Glorious rays of sunshine stormed though the shutters and into Finn's home from the moment the cord was pulled, bathing everything within view of the window in streams of radiant warmth, and on the other side was a picturesque view of the English countryside, complete with verdant trees, lush fields, clear blue sky and a chubby, tattooed face glaring at him through the glass.

'Morning, ol' chum! Mind if we drop in?'

Bollocks! I forgot about the rent!

Finn was startled, and ended up smacking his hip into the corner of his pool table, causing the cup of coffee that he was holding to fly out of his grip, sailing into the other room, where he heard it shatter into pieces. While he staggered around the table, groaning, he picked up the sound of someone stomping their shoes nearby. Since there wasn't a door to stop anyone from coming in, one of the landlord's friends was already inside, kicking the dirt off of his boots and treading it into Finn's carpet. Finn's thoughts blared in the back of his head, telling him not to let them get any further inside, unless they went into the bathroom and found what was dozing off in the bath. All hell would break lose if that happened.

Nearly making it into the next room, Finn was struck on the back of the head, making him drop to his knees. Next, he was forced to the floor, while the landlord moved past the window and entered into his flat, taking up a space beside his accomplice.

'Oi, Lacksley! You look like you got run over by a tractor! Been spending all of my dosh getting yourself stitched back together have ya!?' Simon belched.

Finn gritted his teeth. He had slipped up, and now they had him pinned to the ground and at their mercy.

'I got mugged, alright? That's why I've been late on my payment. If you just give me a minute, I'll—'

Finn couldn't tell which one of them was doing it, but one of them stepped on his head, mashing his face into the carpet. He had barely enough time to turn his head to the side to stop his nose from being crushed.

'Way too late for that! Do you honestly think I give a monkey's about whatever sob story you pull out of your arse! Tell me where the damned money is, or Ted here'll shank ya!'

There was a flick – the definite sound of a switchblade unfolding. It set Finn's teeth on edge.

'Better do as the man says,' came the voice of Ted, a little softer than the growl of his landlord, but still just as intimidating. 'I'd hate to live through gettin' run down by a tractor, just to end up stabbed to bits in my own apartment...'

Finn didn't have the money they wanted, but he had to come up with something, or they would follow through on that threat.

'I... I keep a stash on top of the cupboard, just take it and g—'

This time he could tell it was Simon treading on him, as Ted had gone into the next room. The heel of Simon's boot was being pressed into the square of his back, making him wince from where he had recently been mended.

Craning his neck to see what the landlord's friend was doing, he was upset to see the man tearing out the contents of his shelving, scattering his plates and cups onto the floor where they joined the broken shards of his coffee mug.

'I said it was on top! are you deaf!?'

The man destroying his belongings put all his weight on the cupboard and pulled it off the wall, breaking it apart along with the remaining ceramics inside.

Bloody hell, they're gonna find Eric at this rate! I have to do something!

'I just looked there! You're a bloody liar!' he called back, to which, Simon stepped down a little harder.

Sneering at the prone body of the flat's tenant, Ted made to wander back over, but on his way, he got distracted by the bathroom door. Seeing his eyes drawn to it, Finn started to panic.

'Don't go in there!' He yelled.

Finn's sudden outburst seemed to draw the attention of both of them, who now donned mischievous smirks on their faces.

'Oooh? Why not? What are you hiding, Lacksley boy?'

'Uh… Nothing. That's just the bathroom. There's nothing you want in there…'

Simon bent down and pinched Finn's ear between his pudgy fingers.

'Just the bathroom, eh? And why wouldn't you want us going in? Afraid you left a floater in there?' Simon taunted. His breath stunk.

Saying this turned out to be highly amusing to Ted, who couldn't stop himself from chuckling.

'I'm warning you, don't bloody go in there!'

'Shut it!' the landlord barked. 'Ted, chop-chop'

Ted reached for the door handle, and had just begun turning, when he noticed someone hovering behind the landlord. Someone clad in black: gloved, hooded and wearing a skull-patterned bandana over his mouth and nose, only showing their eyes within the murky depths of their hood. They were yellow.

'Are you terrorizing our pal Finn?'

Simon glanced over his shoulder and peered into the sulphurous eyes of the hooded figure.

'That's our job'

That voice... You've got to be joking...

Simon tilted his head and looked the stranger up and down. When he was done making his inspection, the landlord tutted and puffed himself out, trying to look big and brawny, despite being a head shorter than the towering intruder.

'Yeah? Got a problem with that, do ya? Why don't you shove off and skulk around somewhere else?' Simon spat.

The being inside the hood laughed, deep and wickedly, unzipping it's coat down to the middle.

'Oh, I think we'll skulk around wherever we like... It's in our name, after all...'

As the creature inside gradually emerged from its disguise, Simon's expression turned from smug to utterly terrified, until it finally pulled off its bandana, and he was left staring at the pale, monstrous visage of a creature, more horrifying than anything he had ever seen before. Delighting in the man's fear, the monster's alligator-like jaws split into three, treating him to the sight of more glistening fangs than he could count, before his eyes glazed over, and he fainted to the floor.

Unlike the landlord, his accomplice wasn't so easily frightened, and charged at the hooded monstrosity, bellowing his war-cry and propelling his switchblade out like a spear.

He came to a dead halt when the knife pierced into the monster's abdomen, burying itself up to the hilt, whereby he was grabbed, hard enough that while the blade had slipped all the way in, he couldn't pull it out again.

'Oogh, ouch. I think you got me in the kidney, there.'

The creature pulled the landlord's friend close, so that his piercing, yellow glare encompassed all that he could see, and he made that clicking, rattling sound, which sent Ted into a fit of despair.

'Wh-what the hell are you!?' he yelled.

The skulker grinned, once again exposing his rows of deadly, shining teeth, and turned the man with his knife still dug into him, so that his back was facing towards the entrance to Finn's apartment, where three more figures, wearing the same attire as him were waiting, and then told him, 'Why don't you ask some of my friends, I'm sure that they will be more than happy to show you what we are... Personally...', before thrusting him into them.

Simon's accomplice struggled for a short while, calling out for help madly, while being dragged out of the apartment, where the sound of his voice faded away into nothing.

Not them. I can't go through all of that again!

Ever since Simon had been dealt with, Finn had been transfixed on the appearance of the strangers who had come to his aid. They were a familiar nightmare, come back to haunt him, the kidnappers who had once chased him out of his home, shot at him, hunted him, and taken away Eric, plunging him into a cold and frightening reality where he danced on the edge between life and death, and now they were back, as living products of the horrors that he had endured down below. Returned as skulkers. Trying to crawl away, he just wasn't fast enough, and ended up being blocked by the one who had taken care of his landlord.

'Not planning on jumping out the back window again, are we?' he said, smiling down at him. 'Let me give you a hand.'

The hooded skulker went to bend down, but stopped midway, feeling a painful reminder of what he had allowed to happen to him.

'Oh, right. I almost forgot about this...' he joked, then proceeded to pull the switchblade out of him in one swift movement.

'Yowch! That is nothing like ripping off a plaster! I think he really did puncture a kidney... Anywho, let's get you up on your feet,' he rambled, clutching at his wound, as the red foam started to build up under his hand.

The skulker dressed in black offered out a hand, and Finn, feeling like he had no alternative, took it and allowed himself to be helped back up. Once again, it looked like he had entered into a hopeless situation; there was no doubt more skulkers than he could handle waiting outside if he tried to run, not that he could even do that, as then there would be nobody left to protect Eric. All that was left was to wait for the inevitable, for him to be whisked away and turned into a skulker in some gloomy basement. He could see that happening, but when one of the other skulkers came back with a carrier bag, heavy with some unknown instrument, he started to imagine that they might do it right here.

'There's nowhere to run, Lacksley. We've got a surprise for you...' the kidnapper told him menacingly, clasping a hand over his eyes. 'No peeking... Hey, what's the problem? Surely, it's not that hard to find!'

Finn heard the plastic bag rustling and the sound of one of the skulkers getting stressed.

'Oh, it's in here, he just wedged it right at the bottom, so it's really hard to get out!'

'Ugh! Give it here, bellend! You've got to take the stuff on top out first… Now, hold out your hands, Mr Lacksley.'

Everything had come crashing down. Here, in his own home, he was going to be injected with the serum, and he couldn't even see it happen. Something cold had been placed into his hands, he was sure that it must have been part of a new method for administering the serum, after Eric had told him how it had been given to him. Finn presumed that any minute now, he was going to feel the point of a needle pierce into one of his arms… Any minute now…

'Hey, you can look now.'

Expecting the worst, Finn slowly took in the sight of the object he had been made to hold, which became immediately far less dreadful and infinitely more puzzling once he read out the words printed on its colourful exterior.

'Raspberry… Ice… Cream…?'

One of the hooded skulkers uncurled his tongue from a spiral shape that he was making at the end of his snout, chirping the sound of a party horn.

'Surprise! It might have got a bit melted, but it's still good.'

Finn's mouth opened and closed, and his brow furrowed. he had no words.

'Well, that's actually the gift we got for your pal, Eric. Here's what we got you, a little "going away" present, to remember us by,' the skulker with the bag explained, fishing out a six-pack of beers and placing it on the counter. 'We drank all of your cans the last time we were over, so it's only fair.'

'Yeah... Sorry about that...' another one called to the confused man.

Finn put the tub of ice-cream down next to it, feeling a headache coming on.

'What do you mean "going away"? What's all this about?'

They all shared a look, nodding to each other as if taking part in some wordless conversation, before returning their attention to Finn.

'We're going on holiday to America! Exciting, huh?' The bag holder exclaimed.

Finn blinked.

'Wait... This has got something to do with that doctor, hasn't it?' Finn guessed.

'That's right, he's asked us to be one of the advanced scouting parties he's sending to the US. Shame you can't come with us though...' one of them answered, as they all began to back out of his apartment. '...Doctor Voe is cooking up something special for you, he-he... Almost makes me feel jealous... Well, that's all the time we've got left. We really ought to hit the road, so we'll be seeing you around, Lacksley! Ciao!'

Dragging the landlord away by his legs, the hooded skulkers sneaked through the frame where his front door used to be and out of sight, leaving Finn gawking at the space they had once occupied, quite unsure of how he had survived such an encounter. After making a quick check outside to make sure that they were really gone, Finn walked over to his sink in a daze and splashed some water onto his face.

So, Andrew Voe is already sending his agents out to other countries? Sooner or later there isn't going to be a place left on earth that isn't infested with skulkers... I just hope that none of the people getting turned over there end up like these lot... The last thing I need is a whole continent of one-hundred percent, absolute creeps!

Something made a loud slurping noise beside Finn's ear, nearly making him jump out of his skin, but he soon dropped his guard, coming to the realisation that it was only Eric, who had wandered out of the bathroom, half-dressed and dripping wet, and had sunk his jaws deep inside of the raspberry ice-cream tub. Eric's dilated pupils took in the image of Finn giving him an appraisal, and he carefully withdrew himself from the container. He had got ice-cream all over his head, staining his fine scales a bright purple, rivulets of it flowed off his facial features. Once the end of his nose was out of the tub, he tilted his head towards Finn, looking guilty as can be.

'I... uh... Sorry, I should have asked first.'

Finn pinched the bridge of his nose and shuffled away from the sink, making room so that Eric could wash the mess off. While he was busy cleaning up, Finn explained what had happened during the last few minutes, much to Eric's shock.

'I really slept through all of that? That's... I need to start being more alert, that's just not acceptable...' Eric sobbed.

'Come on, don't put yourself down. It was a wild coincidence.'

'Yeah, but those guys knew where you lived... This place already isn't safe for us to stay, so I should be doing my part to help,' he reasoned, turning off the tap.

Sighing, Finn dug into his pockets, pulling out his lighter and a box of cigs, then made his way back over to the window and leant against the pool table as he pulled the blinds up. Pushing the window back, Finn glanced over, to see that Eric had joined him by the table, giving him a thought.

'You know, we still have a while yet before we need to get going...' Finn pointed out, setting down the box and lighter, and picking up the triangle to go about setting the balls inside of it. 'Have you played before?'

Eric scanned the table, and then smirked, picking out a cue that was leaning on the wall nearby with his good arm.

'I think I'll pick it up as I go,' he stated.

Checking that the triangle was set, Finn noted that Eric would be at a big disadvantage playing with only one arm.

'I'm gonna go easy on you, if you don't mind,' Finn said.

Eric chuckled and positioned himself to strike the white ball with the end of his cue.

'I do mind, if we're going to be leaving soon, then I want to make the most of it. Plus, I want to see what your face looks like when you end up getting thrashed by a one-armed beginner.'

Grabbing his own cue, Finn broke into a smile and lifted the triangle.

'Cheeky sod... Alright, you're on!'

Finn and Eric's game lasted for a good while, and while they played, the fragments of the coffee mug Finn had dropped, protruded from a puddle of brown liquid in the next room. There would be little point in mopping up the shattered Union Jack that lay broken and scattered, reasoning that in the days to come, they would be long gone, and in those days, hiding amongst the forests, and alleyways, and all cold places the world over, would be more razor-sharp teeth and harrowing claws than you could dream of, waiting patiently for their time to strike... In the dead of night...

AUTHOR'S NOTE

Special thanks to Lydie Taupin for the invaluable help and support, as well as being an amazing friend.